KATE TATTERSALL
ADVENTURES IN China

R.S. FLEMING

DCB

Canada Council for the Arts   **Conseil des Arts du Canada**

The publisher gratefully acknowledges the support of the Canada Council for the Arts and the Ontario Arts Council for its publishing program. We acknowledge the financial support of the Government of Canada through the Canada Book Fund (CBF) for our publishing activities, and the Government of Ontario through the Ontario Media Development Corporation, an agency of the Ontario Ministry of Culture, and the Ontario Book Publishing Tax Credit Program.

Library and Archives Canada Cataloguing in Publication

Fleming, R. S., author
Kate Tattersall adventures in China / R.S. Fleming.

Issued in print and electronic formats.
ISBN 978-1-77086-305-7 (pbk.).— ISBN 978-1-77086-307-1 (mobi).—
ISBN 978-1-77086-306-4 (epub)
I. Title.

PS8611.L42K37 2013   jC813'.6   C2013-903676-8
                                              C2013-903677-6

Cover art: Nick Craine
Interior text design: Tannice Goddard, Soul Oasis Networking

Printed and bound in Canada.
Manufactured by Friesens in Altona, Manitoba, Canada in August, 2013.

MIX
Paper from
responsible sources
FSC® C016245

This book is printed on 100% post-consumer waste recycled paper.

DANCING CAT BOOKS
An imprint of Cormorant Books Inc.
10 St. Mary Street, Suite 615, Toronto, Ontario, M4Y 1P9
www.dancingcatbooks.com
www.cormorantbooks.com

For Kaley and Tavish

CONTENTS

MAY 1849, MAYFAIR, WESTMINSTER

Lady Katelyn Elizabeth Beaufort stood still, head up, shoulders back, a slight smile playing upon her lips, eyelids drooping. Her stepmother had taught this sophisticated look to Kate, as her friends and family called her, and she dutifully kept the false visage plastered on her face.

"Thank you for coming, Lord Compton," Lady Jane Beaufort, the Countess Beaufort and Kate's stepmother, said to the splendidly dressed gentleman who stood in the front hall, with its oak panels aglow and marble tiles gleaming. "And you, Lord Ossulston," she added, acknowledging a tall, thin older man.

"Our pleasure, Lady Beaufort," Earl Compton said. He was handsome, with a confident air, perhaps thirty-five years old. "It has been delightful visiting with your husband, and to be in the presence of such accomplished young ladies." He flashed a smile, at Kate in particular.

"Now, that's quite enough," Jane said with a stern tone, but then smiled warmly. "Good day." She curtsied, a quick dip with her short plump body, and a footman opened the door.

Kate copied her stepmother, but did a far deeper, slower, more elegant curtsy, her slender body ideal for such a movement. She knew her exquisite taffeta gown was tailored to show off her statuesque torso, toned shoulders, and long neck.

"Good day," the men said in turn. They bowed, took up their top hats and gloves, and stepped outside.

Once the door was shut, Jane moved to the cards and letters

on the hall table. "So ... what did you think of Earl Compton?" she asked with a raised eyebrow. "You already enchanted the father, now the son is after you too."

Kate pulled the silver comb from her hair and let the long plaits drop.

I wish we were in the country, London is far too busy. Why can't I have some time to myself? To make some friends? She glanced at her stepmother, trying to form a diplomatic response. "He's very nice. I can see he gets his handsome looks from his father, who's a charming man. His work with the Royal Society is very interesting."

"Yes," Jane nodded. "If you married the father you would be a marchioness immediately, and probably a dowager by the age of twenty-five, free to wed again. Marry the son and you'll soon inherit the title." Jane leafed through the various gentlemen's calling cards and mail while talking. "Lord Ossulston is courting Olivia Montagu."

"Oh, yes. I like Olivia. Isn't she nineteen? Lord Ossulston must be about forty. That's quite a lot of years." *I don't want an old husband.*

"Not very many, and a fine match." Jane gathered up the mail and moved towards the stairs.

"Well, perhaps in four years, when I'm nineteen, I'll be able to choose a suitor," Kate said quietly while following her up into the brightly decorated sitting room with its dark red velvet curtains and richly upholstered furniture. *I know what she'll say to that. "Nonsense ..."*

"Nonsense. We've been through this a dozen times. Your presentation to the Queen went ahead this year because of your maturity. You've already reached womanhood in every way, not like these girls who are still developing. You haven't grown any taller since I met you, and a good thing it is too. I'm certain you'll just fill out a bit when you have children. No, you should be engaged by next year. It would be ideal if you let yourself be wooed before your journey, so a prospective husband is ready to propose when you return."

"But I leave in a fortnight."

"It's enough time for a kiss and a promise."

"Why would a man wait for me like that?"

"Ha!" Jane threw her hands up, waving the mail. "Look at all these invitations. Kate, I've told you before, you're a classic beauty. You're just what men want, striking features, large lustrous eyes, a Grecian profile. Now that I've refined you, changed you from a tomboy ... well, you're quite possibly the most desirable debutante of the season."

"You're exaggerating."

"Mmm, perhaps a bit. Of course the voluptuous blondes are popular. They were in my day, too, but most of them bleach their hair, leaving it dull, not sleek like yours. You're getting a great deal of attention, I'm sure. Keeping your face out of the sun for a couple of years has your alabaster skin contrasting nicely with your onyx hair."

"Alabaster and onyx? What am I, a statue? When did you come up with that? Don't you think fair skin and black hair is more accurate?"

"Oh, they're just words that mean the same thing. I like describing you as alabaster and onyx when I'm talking to men who haven't met you yet."

"What? Mother, who? Who have —"

"Everyone. And you generally have a sweet disposition, as long as that temper is kept in check."

Kate looked down at this woman, who'd only come into her life two years ago, trying to control her anger. *You've brought such change. Father was fine as a widower for thirteen years. We had fun together.* "It's not fair, Mother, expecting me to select an elderly gentleman when I'm fifteen. You married Father at twenty-three."

"Yes, and he was fifty-two," Jane retorted, taking a seat. "And you know I was previously engaged at sixteen, married at seventeen, and there were complications involved. Everyone has different circumstances. With your rank you have greater responsibilities to consider. Has there been no one you deemed suitable?"

Kate perched on a sofa, afraid to say. She sensed her insides tighten. "What would you think of a younger man?"

"Ah-ha!" Jane clapped her hands and grinned. "It's the Marquess of Chandos you're considering!"

"I am not!" Kate snapped, angry at the way her stepmother had reacted. *Stop treating this like a silly guessing game. You've been badgering me for weeks.* "Perhaps someone who is about twenty?"

"That would be very unusual," Jane said bluntly, and frowned, looking deflated. "An older husband is less demanding, and not as likely to have mistresses."

"Yes, yes." Kate glanced out the window, embarrassed by her stepmother's candour. "Please don't go on and on about such matters."

"You must have someone in mind."

"No, I don't." Kate felt herself getting hot. She pressed on through clenched teeth, "I've put up with all these society requirements to please you and Father, but I'm not ready to court anyone."

"Keep control of your temper," Jane growled back, jumping to her feet.

"I am in control," Kate said slowly, rising and towering over her stepmother. She stared down at her with arms crossed. "And I'm —"

Suddenly a maid came into the room with a tray of sweets and tea. Kate unfolded her arms and tried to smile, while Jane turned and strolled to a bookshelf.

"Are ya quite well, muh lady? You're all flushed."

"Yes, I'm fine, thank you," Kate responded. *Deep breaths, calm down.*

"Where would ya like this?" the maid asked.

"The table in the corner, please," Jane said without turning around.

The maid quickly placed the tray and scampered from the room. Jane drifted to the table and took up a tart. Kate could tell her stepmother was cooling off and peering at her sideways.

"All right, Kate," Jane said gently, returning to her seat, cradling a cup and saucer. "Perhaps when you return from your voyage you'll be ready."

Oh, that was an abrupt change. Kate perched on the sofa again. "Yes, perhaps. I'm looking forward to travelling with my brother. Jack has been promising me some kind of a grand tour for years."

"Most girls your age would prefer France and Switzerland, then the ancient countries. Italy and Greece are extremely interesting."

"We'll be going through Egypt."

"I'm afraid it may be terribly uncivilized."

"That's part of the adventure." Kate let her eyes wander to the atlas she had been leafing through earlier. *I wish we were setting out today; I can't wait to get away.*

"Oh, you and your adventures! I had so hoped you would outgrow such notions." Jane stumped over to the sweets and selected a biscuit. "Your grandfather knows all the best society in the major ports of India, but to go all the way to China, where we don't know anybody, seems excessive."

"Jack has a friend at the port of Canton."

"Your brother has a friend? Where would he find the time? All he does is tinker in that odious workshop."

"He has many friends," Kate insisted, knowing there was some venom between her stepmother and brother. "Mostly through the Royal Society. Do you remember the physician who spoke at the fundraising tea we attended last month? About his work in China?" *With wavy blond hair, clear grey eyes, nice smile, and pleasant manner?*

"That remarkably young doctor? He's a friend of your brother?"

"Indeed, Henry Tattersall. He's been a friend of Jack's for about three years."

"Dr. Tattersall ..." Jane said quietly, and rolled her eyes around the room. "Obviously very intelligent ... he's the son of a gentleman? Ah, yes ... a Hyde Park Corner Tattersall, extremely wealthy ..."

"Yes," Kate nodded. "The very same."

"Well, Jack surprises me. Good for him. And it's nice that he would make time for a commoner."

"Isn't it?" Kate said happily, glad with the way the conversation was progressing. *When I met him the whole room went cloudy. If I daydream about the moment it's all a blur.*

"I remember he spoke about his work in China, saving natives and Europeans from all the odd illnesses."

"Yes, he's been out there for just over a year, after he finished schooling at only eighteen!"

"That is young to earn a diploma."

"Jack told me he answered every question put to him by quoting known experts. He made references to treatises and books written by the physicians administering the examinations."

"He must be very clever, but it would be a challenge for him to find patients in England with so little experience. He's gone back to the Far East already?"

"He was only home for a month for speaking engagements, to raise money for his work, but I believe his father actually looks after all expenses, including the clinic in Canton."

"Ah, a papa who coddles his son. I suppose he could buy him a thriving established practice here, or whatever he desires. Rather reminds me of your relationship with your father."

"He's very good to me."

"Yes, he indulges you in many ways, too much so. Now, whether you're going to accept a courtship or not, you still have to receive callers until you leave. It's odd for you to sail before the season is over, but that may add to your allure ... Yes, very clever, in fact." Jane stepped away to where she had placed the mail. "And there's all this correspondence to which you must respond, and you shall accept some of these invitations."

"Of course," Kate agreed with enthusiasm, feeling the excitement of her impending voyage. "I've been putting my letters off. I'll tend to them now."

"Very good, and I'll speak to Lord Beaufort about inviting the Comptons to dinner." Jane swept out of the room.

Kate sat at an occasional desk and started going through her mail, trying to be diligent, but it proved difficult to concentrate on the messages. Taking a fresh sheet of paper, she dipped her pen, then practised a signature in flowing script.

"Mrs. Dr. Henry Tattersall." *Oh, that looks lovely.* She tried again. "Lady Katelyn Elizabeth Tattersall." *How elegant, absolutely splendid, but if I take his name I'll have to give up my title. Hmm.* "Mrs. Kate Tattersall." *Yes, that's fine. Just an ordinary wife. I wonder if I could help him at his infirmary?* She stared out the window. *I guess he would have to propose first ... he hardly knows I exist ...*

The doors rolled open with a thump and Mrs. Farewell, Kate's childhood nanny and the current housekeeper of the family's London house, entered with a vase of flowers. The short, stocky woman had round shoulders and a rolling walk, and often hummed as she patrolled about the halls.

"Hello, child," she said, upon noticing Kate watching her.

"How old were you when you got married?" Kate asked, coming straight from her thoughts to the question.

"Which time? I've outlived two husbands."

"Really? Mr. Farewell is your third?"

"Indeed, child."

"The first, then. How old were you?"

"Fourteen, but those were different times. He went a soldier an' never came back. Died fighting the Frenchies in Spain."

"I'm sorry. I never knew. How old was he?"

"Oh, hmm ... sixteen or seventeen. He was so handsome, an' strong ..."

Kate watched as her old nanny got a faraway look on her face, the wrinkles softening and all expression fading. She waited quietly for a moment, then asked softly, "And did you have children?"

Mrs. Farewell returned from her reverie, smiling and squinting, apparently inspecting for dust.

"Yes, a tiny creature. He lived just long enough to be christened."

"Goodness, I'm sorry again," Kate said looking down, surprised by how plainly Mrs. Farewell had put such a sad occurrence.

"Now, child, infants are taken all the time, straight to heaven. Don't be gloomy for me. Your mother lost three boys at birth."

"True ... but that doesn't make it easier, the thought of having a baby die ... And your second husband?"

"I'd just turned twenty when I met a widower, with five children. He was about forty. Died of Irish fever a few years later. So did the two youngest girls. It was after the others grew up I came to work for your family."

"That part I can tell," Kate said. "I had a nursemaid for a while, but then —"

"All right, let's not waste words on what we both know. Get back to your work, an' I'll get back to mine." She moved off into the hall, humming quietly.

Looking back at the pile of letters, Kate focused and started reading quickly. She would send regrets to most of the invitations, polite responses to the inquiries about her health, and thanks to all the wishes for a safe journey. Suddenly, she found herself reading an unusual note. It was written in short sentences and a spidery hand, and requested she come to the office for Foreign Affairs in two days' time, signed Lord Palmerston.

I don't remember meeting him. Was he the man who trod on my toes at the Nelsons' ball? No, that was Lord Paget. Palmerston ... I don't believe he's attended any of the social events. Foreign Affairs ... he must want to discuss our voyage? Perhaps they do this whenever members of the nobility travel to far-off lands? I shall attend to this request.

She wrote back feeling quite mature.

Imagine, me in a meeting in the Foreign Office. This will be exciting.

CHAPTER 2

FOREIGN OFFICE
DOWNING STREET, WESTMINSTER

Kate stepped from her carriage, a footman in light green livery offering his hand and holding the door. The roofs of the landau were folded down, providing a wide open view, so she'd already observed that Whitehall and Downing Street, the heart of British government, seemed to be frequented only by men. She stood in front of the Foreign Office and hesitated.

"Wait for me here, please," she said to the driver.

Men, mostly in top hats, dark coats, grey or fawn trousers, and light-coloured waistcoats, moved past on the pavement. Kate wore a shimmering gold suit, a lavishly decorated sun hat (brightly coloured silk flowers circling the crown), a very lacy high-collared shirt, and cream kidskin gloves, and carried a small handbag with intricate silver and gold embroidery. The sun reflected off her ensemble.

I'm out of place. I should have worn brown or black ... and asked my father to come with me. Kate perceived men were trying not to ogle her, but failing. Some stopped, seemingly to chat with each other, and casually glanced in her direction. *I feel like a lamb amongst wolves! I should have brought my maid.* The uncomfortable feeling provided by their attention served as an ideal spur to hurry up the steps and into the building. The carriage attendant scrambled to open the door for her. The dark interior masked the glow of her fine clothes. *Whew, this is better.*

"I don't know how long this will take," she said to her servant.

"I'll wait by the doors, my lady."

In the entrance hall stood a reception desk.

"Good morning." The clerk rose on her approach. "How may I assist you?"

"I'm Lady Katelyn Beaufort," Kate said, presenting an embossed calling card and trying to sound confident, assuming her sophisticated false face. "I have an appointment with Lord Palmerston at ten o'clock."

"Very good, my lady." The clerk bowed. "This way, please."

He led her up a flight of stairs to a large hall. At the far end stood another desk and another clerk. Kate followed slowly, taking in her surroundings. *I must remember not to lick my lips.* She had applied some glossy carmine pomade to accentuate her mouth with a rosy colour, and also a bit of black paint to the base of her eyelashes.

"This is Lady Katelyn," the first clerk said to the second, passing over Kate's calling card. He then disappeared back down the stairs.

"Please have a seat, me lady," the clerk said, indicating any number of chairs that lined the hall.

"Thank you, but I'll stand." Kate moved to a painting, a large battle scene, and pretended to examine the brush strokes. *How do people make paint come to life?* For years her governess had continually attempted to hone Kate's artistic skill, but while she found sketching enjoyable, the ability to render finer work eluded her. *I hope I don't have to wait too long. This is quite intimidating, not at all what I was expecting. I definitely should have asked Father to come with me.* She stood nervously fiddling with the strings on her handbag. Remembering her society training she stopped that fidgeting, but then adjusted the cameo brooch pinned at her throat distractedly. Catching herself again, she forced her free hand to her side just as the large dark door at the end of the hall opened. Three men strode out and hurried off.

"Step in here please, me lady." The clerk held the door for her.

Gliding gracefully into the room, acting more confident than she felt, Kate found herself in a grand office of yellowed oak and dark leather.

"Me lawd, the Lady Katelyn Elizabeth Beaufort, daughter of Lawd Beaufort," the clerk said in a strong, clear voice with a haughty accent.

Lord Palmerston rose from behind a capacious desk to greet her. A large man well past middle age, white haired with cheeks covered by grizzled whiskers, he wore rather formal attire of black and grey.

"Me lady, Lawd Henry John Temple, the third Viscount Palmerston, Secretary of State for Foreign Affairs." Having finished the introductions the clerk silently left the room.

"Won't you sit down? You're styled Lady Kate, aren't you? May I call you Lady Kate?"

"Yes, of course, Lord Palmerston." Kate took a seat in front of his desk. *Pooh, I've got some hair falling around my cheeks. And my nose is itchy.*

"I'm a man of few words, except in Parliament," Palmerston said while taking his seat. "And I have other engagements this morning, so I will be brief."

"Oh, very good." *I'd like to keep this short.* "Why have you asked me here today?" Kate asked briskly.

"It's the matter I broached with your brother," Palmerston said, wide-eyed. "He suggested you to me."

"He did?" *This must be about Foreign Affairs.* "In regards to our voyage?"

"Yes ... your voyage. Have you discussed it with your brother recently?"

"Not since last month." Kate smiled. "We'll be sailing to Egypt, travelling overland to Suez, then on to —"

"Yes, yes." Palmerston waved a hand about. "But your brother must have told you about China."

"Oh, ah, yes ... we're going to visit a friend of his in Canton."

"You are? Whom?"

"A doctor, Mr. Henry Tattersall."

"Indeed?" Palmerston sat forward and peered closely at Kate. "An extremely intelligent young man. And you'll aid him in his taskings?"

Kate didn't know how to respond. *Taskings? What's that?*

"Didn't Jack mention anything about a mission?" Palmerston added and stared at her intently.

She felt surprised. How odd to hear her brother, the Viscount, referred to by his first name outside their family circle. At the same moment Kate thought she understood. "The Church of England Mission at Ningpo? We're ferrying two crates of Bibles there for the Waldegraves."

"No," Palmerston said. "Not that kind of mission. I'm referring to a clandestine operation. Didn't your brother mention it?"

Clandestine operation? I'm starting to feel stupid. I've never heard of such a thing. Kate paused, feeling muddled, wishing she wasn't in this confusing conversation. "Lord Palmerston, you ... you have me at a complete and utter loss."

"This is all rather awkward," the old man said. "Over the years I have sometimes struggled to communicate with your brother."

Kate found herself even more puzzled. "You've met with Jack for years?" She studied the politician, trying to interpret his frown and sagging whiskers, which made him look like a grumpy bear.

"Yes, we meet, occasionally." Palmerston rose. "And I believe you should talk with him before we have any further discourse."

Kate stood as well. She sensed her insides constrict. *This is quite grave. Is he angry with me?* "Have I done something wrong?"

"No, Lady Kate. I fear it's your brother who is delinquent. Talk to him about your voyage."

"All right."

Palmerston walked to the door, but stopped and turned without opening it. "You assay all Jack's infernal devices? You've mastered them?"

"Well ... yes," she said weakly. *That's supposed to be a secret.*

It was true: as long as Kate could remember she had tested everything her brother built. In fact, her suggestions inspired Jack, and she often aided with improvements.

"His weapons too?" Palmerston pressed. "You never miss a shot?"

"That's a bit much." *How embarrassing.* "I'm a lady, in more than title now. I came out last month and have to consider my reputation. Is there truly a need to discuss my marksmanship?"

"I wouldn't if it weren't relevant. Aren't you rather old for coming out? How old are you — nineteen? Twenty?"

Twenty! This outfit must make me look quite adult, or perhaps it's the bit of cosmetics. "I'm actually —"

"Let me assure you, whatever is spoken between us is in the strictest confidence," Palmerston said quickly, checking his time-piece. "Are you a sharpshooter?"

"Yes," Kate allowed reluctantly. "My father says I'm the best shot he's ever seen."

"Lord Beaufort taught you to shoot?"

"Yes. Guns, rifles, and pistols, with both hands." *And how to use a sabre, but let's keep that quiet at least.*

"And you are gifted with languages, aren't you?"

"Certainly." *That I can speak proudly of, as an accomplished lady.* "They were a large part of my education. French and German, of course, but also Latin, Spanish, and I'm still learning Russian. A smattering of other tongues, too."

"Excellent!" Palmerston opened the door. "Thank you for coming today. Please discuss matters with your brother as soon as possible, Lady Kate." He bowed.

Kate, realizing his action was meant as a dismissal, quickly curtsied, then stepped from the office, the door thumping behind her. *Hrumpf, he shouldn't have sent me off like that. Discuss what matters with Jack? I'm still lost. This has all been completely mystifying ...*

CHAPTER 3

HASTINGS

The day for leaving London started at dawn. Kate wept upon saying goodbye to her father and stepmother; however, her emotions were mixed. She was saddened by the separation, but excited about the voyage. She made the trip with her lady's maid, Isabel, and Mrs. Farewell. They went first to Brighton by train, then hired a coach for the ride to the coastal town of Hastings.

The expectation of travelling with her brother had Kate bubbling over, everything amusing. Although there were sixteen years between them they were very close, all their other siblings having died as children. Jack and his family lived in a grand new red brick house near a church, and the inventor kept a cavernous workshop by the docks.

When the coach rolled up in front of the house, Jack's wife, Phoebe, came from the front door with her children, three-year-old Jack and toddler Connie.

"Hello, how are you?" Kate called from the coach window.

"We're all fine," Phoebe replied while approaching the front gate. "How was London?"

"Tiring. You know I'd rather not be in town. Our Somersetshire estate is where I belong."

The coach guard opened the door. Kate climbed down and ran to her sister-in-law for a hug.

"Careful," Phoebe laughed, "I'm about eight months along." She held her distended belly, her usually fine proportions hidden by a bulky pinafore.

Phoebe's rosy cheeks, round blue eyes, and piled mouse-brown hair provided a plain, healthy look. Kate loved her sister-in-law and knew her as a steady, honest, and caring woman. When newlywed, five years ago, Jack and Phoebe had lived at Quantock Hall for a while and it was a happy memory from Kate's childhood. She stooped and kissed her niece and nephew.

"The baby will be over eight months old before we get back from our tour," Kate speculated.

"We?" Phoebe cocked her head. "You don't mean Jack. You know he's decided not to go."

"Pardon? What?!" Kate straightened and felt her head spin. "Not to go? When did he decide this?"

"A few weeks ago. I thought he wrote you."

"No, he didn't. Where is he?" Kate was hot all over. *The inconsiderate, thoughtless man! I wasted my time packing and coming here? All my hopes and dreams of seeing the sights, and going to Egypt, India, China, and visiting Dr. Tattersall ... I'm going to cry.* "Where's Jack?"

"At his shop," Phoebe said softly. "Take a deep breath, Kate. You look ill."

"I'm not ill," she said lightly, trying not to let her upset show any further. "I just need to have a few words with your dear husband. I'll be back soon. Isabel, please look after our baggage."

Kate stormed down to the workshop. She marched over the side rails and past the boatyards to the brick warehouse Jack had adapted to tinker away at his various projects. Entering through the office, she found her brother at his desk, working on a sketch. The salty smell of the seaside was quickly displaced by the poisonous atmosphere wafting from the shop, an acrid mix of burnt oil, wood finishes, and smoke. Kate slammed the door and stood staring at his back, with crossed arms and narrowed eyes, trying to convey her displeasure. Normally she would be happy to be visiting, eager to see Jack's progress with his various inventions and keen to get into the shop, but today she just skimmed the office, taking in the piles of books and drawings scattered about the various tables and desks.

"Grrr, Jack!" Kate barked.

"Oh, hello, Kat," the inventor said quietly. "How are you?"

"Don't call me that, I stopped using it two years ago! I've just seen Phoebe, she says we're not going?" Kate formed it as a question, but it was more like an accusation.

"I'm not going." Jack continued drawing. "Nothing is stopping you."

"Pardon?"

"You go, but I've some taskings I want you to do for me."

Taskings? Palmerston used that word! "Jack? Look at me!"

Her brother set down his pencil and swivelled slowly on his stool. He peered at her with a frown and chewed his bottom lip, one eyebrow raised, his spectacles riding crookedly on the furls of his forehead, his shaggy brown hair dishevelled.

"I met with Lord Palmerston," Kate continued. "You talked to him about me?"

"Yes, I —"

"You told him I'm a master with all your creations?"

"Perhaps, when —"

"Did you say I'm a sharpshooter?"

"Well, you —"

"Why? What's this all about?"

"It's nothing to get distraught over." He rose and started working at his drafting table.

"I'm distraught! Distraught close to bursting!"

"Keep control of your temper," Jack advised gently.

"How am I to go on this tour without you?"

"Take Mrs. Farewell. She can have my passage, and she's tougher than me."

"But she's never left England. I've never been farther than Paris."

"So?" Jack shrugged. "Grandfather's going to meet you on the other side of Egypt. You'll be fine. Besides, I'm no traveller. I don't want to leave England, and Phoebe is close to childbirth."

"But you promised me." Kate felt exhausted. She tore off her bonnet and dashed it onto a desk, allowing the heat to rise from her head. She noticed Jack watching her, trying to form a sentence. "Out with it," she ordered.

"I always said you would go on a grand tour one day. I didn't specifically say I would take you."

"That's not true, Jack. You led me to believe ... it's not the way I understood."

"Whatever. You've got the opportunity to go. How long have you dreamt of travel and adventure?"

Kate had to think for a moment. "Probably all my life."

"Well then?"

"Yes, well then." Kate tossed her head and pursed her lips, starting to feel determined. *I should go. Can I convince Nanny to accompany me? Wait, there are other issues.* "Why do you meet with Lord Palmerston?"

"Oh, I work for Pam."

"Pam? You call Lord Palmerston 'Pam'? And he calls you Jack. You're quite chummy."

"No, no, it's a business relationship."

"Business?"

"He buys my inventions."

"He does? Which ones?"

"Mostly pistols, and my inverto camera obscuras too. It's another reason I cannot go, I have a business commitment with Pam. But this is all secret, you mustn't tell anyone."

Kate was starting to lose track of all the information. *He's been selling his work to Foreign Affairs? It's secret? I've got to get this sorted out.* "What are these taskings?"

"Whilst you're visiting the Chinese ports, take images of all the new buildings other nations are constructing."

"Is that all?"

"Try to do it without anyone noticing."

"I believe I could manage."

"And I have a missive for Henry Tattersall. You don't mind delivering it, do you?"

"Of course not."

"And ..."

"Yes, what else?"

"I need you to take one of my long-range rifles with you, and convey it with the letter to Tattersall."

"Why would a doctor want a rifle? For hunting?"

"Yes, something like that."

"He was just home last month. Why didn't you give it to him then?"

"Ah ... I was still making adjustments."

"Oh. Well, I don't see a problem. Perhaps I can teach him how to handle it?"

"Yes, capital idea." Jack nodded, then glanced at Kate with a half smile. "What a nice opportunity to go for a walk with him? Spend some time together?"

"I ... I would enjoy that ... I mean, it would be pleasant to chat with such an intelligent young gentleman." *Oh, pooh. Jack sees right through me.*

"Good. So, we'll pack you a chest tomorrow afternoon. In the morning I'd like to spend an hour doing some shooting. Would you?"

Kate knew he meant for them to go out in the countryside and test his weapons. She enjoyed doing this, but wanted to be clear how upset she was, so gave him a dark look. "Perhaps, but only if Mrs. Farewell agrees to escort me. Everything hinges on her now."

Still angry, Kate slammed the office door and marched back to the house. *I don't understand. When I met with Palmerston he must have known Jack wasn't going. What else would he have talked to me about? These ... these taskings? Is that a word?*

Shouldn't it be tasks? Upon entering the front door, she discerned movement somewhere nearby. "Mrs. Farewell?"

"Yes, I'm here, child."

"Mrs. Farewell." Kate smiled and approached her old nanny in a back hall near the kitchen, the aroma of fresh bread filling the air. "May I have a word with you?"

"Yes?" the short, stocky woman said slowly with a raised eyebrow.

"You always know when I want something, don't you." Kate smiled brighter.

"I know you better than you know yourself."

"I would very much like for you to come along with me on my journey."

"What? Oh my goodness, child! Me? Leave England?"

"Yes, my brother cannot go," Kate said softly, to sound apologetic. "I must have a chaperone. Please, Nanny. It's all up to you." Her vision started to blur. *This is it. I'll weep for a week if she says no.*

"Here, take my handkerchief," Mrs. Farewell offered.

"I'm fine." Kate wiped the tears away with her hands. "Please, just make a decision."

There was a long pause, the only sound a scullery maid or cook in the kitchen.

"Of course I can't say no," the woman muttered.

"Thank you, Nanny, thank you!" Kate gave her a hug, bending over and clinging to the woman's strong, rounded shoulders.

"All right, that's enough." She pushed away and swatted Kate with the handkerchief. "Mind, I'm in charge now."

"Yes, of course, Nanny." Kate beamed at her, trying to show appreciation.

"What will the Earl and Countess say? They expect me back in two or three days."

"I'll write them, explaining what's happened. If anything, they'll be upset with Jack. Isabel can return tomorrow and deliver the letter. Since you'll be along I don't require my maid. Most of my wardrobe I can manage on my own. This will be like when I was a little girl, and we did everything together!"

"I'll have to buy some more clothes. I only have two outfits."

"Yes, I'll buy whatever you need. We'll go shopping now, and tomorrow you'll have time to pack and get anything else you think of. This will be fun. We'll have a marvellous journey."

"Hmm." Mrs. Farewell didn't seem convinced. "We'll see, child. All in good time.

A VALLEY OUTSIDE OF HASTINGS

The next morning after breakfast, Kate followed Jack to his work-shop, wearing a sun hat and grey walking suit. She was still miffed with her brother and said very little, but couldn't tell if he noticed her ire. Jack wore his usual outfit: a woven brown suit, cap, and boots, but added cloth gaiters that covered him from knees to ankles. The siblings collected the gun cases that were ready just inside the office door, then strolled to the valley, which always served as the firearms testing ground. As they walked, the sun shining down, a beautiful soft morning, Kate forgot her anger and started thinking about what she had learned yesterday.

"Jack?" she ventured. "You sell your pistols to Lord Palmerston?"

"Yes."

"Is he a collector?"

"No, they're for his operatives."

"Foreign Affairs operatives?"

"Yes, that's right."

"Why do they need pistols?"

"For protection."

"Oh, interesting ..." *And rather confusing. Protection from whom? It must be the diplomatic corps who travel to dangerous places ... Maybe I should have a pistol for my voyage?*

Jack had several weapons he wanted his sister to test for him. Although Kate kept it quiet in polite society, she felt quite proud of being a fantastic shot, her large bright eyes providing keen vision. She believed they were her defining feature, and cherished them.

"Now," Jack began as he opened one of the cases, "I have here three variations of my revolvers. Two of these you've fired before."

· Kate thought the weapons were magnificent, some of a brass colour, others silver, with dark wooden handles.

"I see you adopted my last suggestions on this one." Kate smiled, hefting a small model with a casing around the percussion cap chambers.

"Indeed." Jack nodded and pushed his spectacles up on his forehead. "Your hinge and clasp idea for faster reloading was ingenious."

"Thank you."

"Go ahead, try them."

The pistols were a bit cumbersome with five rotating barrels. She tried each, letting the smoke clear between shots, switching hands or using both hands, while her brother squinted through his spectacles at the target: a log twenty paces away.

"These are all vastly superior to your early models," Kate declared. "Have any of them shattered?"

"No," Jack said quietly, looking at his feet.

Two years ago a pistol had exploded in Kate's hand, tearing open her thumb, a wound that took months to fully heal.

"I didn't bring it up to make you feel poorly," Kate said airily. "It's a reasonable query about your progress, that's all." She set down a pistol and massaged her wrist. "I'm getting sore. You know, I think they would make better rifles, Jack. They're so front heavy. Just make them longer and add another handle."

"Hmm, yes, well, they don't have rifled barrels, just straight grooves, but I know what you mean. Rifling is the next step, though." Jack scribbled in his notebook. "I have to concentrate on pistols for the operatives. Usually they need to be able to hide the weapons under their coats when they're in theatre."

"Ah, we're back to the operatives again. In theatre?" Kate asked, perplexed.

"That means on a mission," Jack explained. "You know, like soldiers go into the field or on campaign."

Kate looked at the bulk of the pistol she was holding, then at her slender body, and pondered how she would hide it. *I'd have to put this somewhere in my skirt. Oh my, it must weigh half a stone!* "And Foreign Affairs operatives are already using these in theatre?" Kate asked, pleased with herself for using *operatives* and *theatre* in the same sentence, but Jack didn't seem to be listening.

"Since you've brought up rifles, how about trying this one again?" He opened a case containing a weapon that broke down into three pieces: a long-range rifle.

"Oh, Jack, I don't like that one," Kate moaned. "Every time I fire it I get a bruised shoulder and a black eye."

"Yes, but this is what you'll be delivering to Tattersall, so you need to test my improvements. You've made some astounding shots with it. Please try."

Kate spread out a blanket on a bit of high ground, then eased herself down into a prone position. She admired the brass telescope, silver metalwork, and highly shone cherry wood stock and butt.

"It is a beautiful piece of craftsmanship," she said over her shoulder.

Propped up on her elbows, the cut of her jacket interfering a bit, she loaded the rifle. Kate observed that the ammunition, something else Jack experimented with, appeared different than before.

"This is much better," she said, feeling the cold solid metal of the self-contained cartridge. "Easier to work with."

"Yes, I based them on your suggestions, and a French fellow's design. And I'm experimenting with a new compound called guncotton. It produces hardly any smoke!"

"Interesting."

Previously the round, charge, and percussion cap had been separate; now they were cased together. The breech of the rifle seemed entirely new, the bullet merely sliding in through a spring-loaded covering when the chamber lever was pulled open. Staring down the telescope that ran parallel along the top of the barrel, Kate cocked the hammer, controlled her breathing, picked a tree branch, and fired. The impact slammed into her body, and her head jerked away from the weapon. Kate felt pain start to throb from her shoulder, and her cheek went numb.

"Ow! I thought it wasn't going to kick as much?" *Hrumpf, I guess that isn't part of the improvements.*

"Did you hit what you were aiming at?" Jack ignored her question.

Kate sighted down the telescope again — the branch was gone. "Yes," she confirmed. "One less tree branch down in the valley. Hmm, but about a foot lower than I aimed. I must not have adjusted the telescope properly."

"Excellent! That must be half a mile!"

Kate couldn't help but smile at her brother's enthusiasm and exaggeration. "I would say six hundred yards, perhaps," she said, getting to her feet. "This would be excellent for hunting."

"Yes, and Pam says there could be applications for it."

"For Foreign Affairs?"

"I believe so, yes. Try reloading quickly and firing again."

"Oh, well, I suppose I have a swollen cheek now anyway."

Kate got back into a prone position, worked the lever to empty the breech, slid the next round in, closed the handle, and fired without taking careful aim. Again, the weapon pounded her shoulder, but she kept her face clear. Kate started the process anew, when off to her right she noticed three men in brown country suits. They all carried weapons hooked in their elbows.

"This isn't a hunting season," Kate observed. "Perhaps they're out shooting rabbits?"

"Who?"

"There are men with guns looking at us from the edge of the forest. About two hundred and fifty paces off. Not at the bottom of the valley. From the woods to the northwest."

"Indeed?" Jack squinted around. He then quickly started packing his weapons. "Are they coming this way?"

"Um, yes. Now they're coming." Kate spun on the blanket and sighted through the telescope. "They're just ordinary-looking men."

"Time to go!" Jack ordered, frantically slamming the cases shut.

"Why?" The telescope allowed her clear sight of the men, right down to their whiskers and buttons. "They look like gentlemen farmers."

"We mustn't take any chances." He pulled Kate to her feet. "Come on! Let's get back to town."

Looking into his eyes, Kate saw fear, and she felt her heart thump hard in her throat. *God's wounds, this is really serious!* Leaving the blanket, grabbing cases, Kate cradled the rifle and gathered her skirt, then they ran from the field. *Good thing I'm wearing practical boots.* Entering the low lane, having the security of stone walls on both sides was welcome, and they slowed a bit. Glancing back every few paces, struggling with her load, Kate started feeling dizzy. *Breathe. I've got to breathe. This jacket is too tight. Thank goodness I'm not wearing a corset. I wish I were wearing trousers.* She started falling behind.

"Jack, we need to stow the rifle," she gasped.

"Yes, I'll do it. You keep watch."

Kate dropped everything and leaned on a wall, undoing buttons, looking back. Jack quickly disassembled the rifle and put it in its case.

"Why ... why, Jack? What's this all about?"

"You know we've always kept my inventions secret."

"Yes, I guess so. But I never knew why. And I never really

thought about it. I imagined you were just waiting until they were perfect before offering them for sale."

"They're for the exclusive use of Pam and his operatives. Foreign nations would like to steal them."

"I'm absolutely shocked. So you believe those men would have taken your weapons by force? Do you live with this threat all the time? Are Phoebe and the children safe?"

"Yes, Hastings is secure, I assure you. The valley must have been identified and watched somehow. That's all."

"That's all? How can you be so nonchalant?"

"Because I know what's involved. And I know Pam will deal with this. Don't worry, and don't say anything to Phoebe. In fact, don't ever say anything to anyone. Now, let's go."

Kate gathered her skirt and picked up the cases. "I feel weak, Jack. I think I'm in shock. Are we going to the authorities? Isn't there a garrison of soldiers?"

"Yes. Don't worry. It will be reported and tended to. Remember, not a word to anyone."

Jack ran towards town, Kate doing her best to keep up, fighting her petticoats. Naturally athletic, once she found a pace and with her jacket undone she matched her brother's speed. Upon reaching the cottages on the edge of town, they could see people going about their daily business, chatting and smiling.

"Jack, wait," Kate said coming to a stop. "I must ... I think we're safe now. I must sort myself out."

"Yes, all's right now. Look, here's a bench. Set the cases down for a moment." He took off his cap and fanned himself.

Kate recovered her composure, neatened her hair, smoothed her skirt, and buttoned the jacket tight against her heaving breast. *I'm going to have my next suits cut with more room.*

The siblings continued walking. Kate noticed perspiration working out through the layers of silk and started to feel more comfortable. Her heart and breathing calmed, but she suffered pangs in her stomach. Jack seemed unperturbed, whistling and merrily greeting townsfolk they passed. For Kate it seemed absolutely unreal to be surrounded by a busy happy town, on a beautiful day, after being so frightened by her brother's reaction to the situation.

Leaving the weapons secured in the office of the workshop, she proceeded to the house and ordered a bath, while Jack went off to report to whoever needed to know. Kate talked for a few moments with Phoebe, whom she located in the kitchen yard with her children, then stepped through the rooms of the house. She found each quiet and undisturbed. Finally feeling safe, Kate climbed into a hot tub in a sun-infused room for a long soak.

Sitting on her bed, slipping on fresh silk hose and chemise, Kate combed out her wet hair. Her hands started to shake. *What if Jack had been there by himself? He's so nearsighted he wouldn't have seen their approach.* She recalled the faces and clothes of the men. *They looked like ordinary English gentlemen farmers. Who were they? Would they have murdered us? For Jack's weapons?* Despite the warmth of the day Kate felt a sudden chill. She pulled on some long wool stockings and a cashmere robe. *I should get dressed and have something to eat. Yes, food will make me feel better ... but I'm not hungry.* Lying down, she closed her eyes and took some long, slow, calming breaths. *I hope I'm never in a situation like that again.*

JACK'S WORKSHOP

Kate sauntered down to Jack's workshop feeling better, having had a nap and a meal. The day was now quite warm, a salty breeze blew off the ocean, seagulls reeled overhead, and the dock-yards were busy. Broad-shouldered navvies, hard men attired in patched clothes and heavy boots, toiled away on the latest rail bed. Kate noticed them stop their work and watch her glide by in her light pink suit with matching gloves and parasol. This outfit was made to shimmer in the sunlight, with fine lace trimmings. She'd decided not to wear a hat, and her hair, still damp, tumbled down her back, around her shoulders, and curled over her breast. Normally she would have paid the labourers no heed, but after the morning's trauma she felt glad to graciously nod at them and have the men smile and wave back.

Upon entering Jack's office she found it empty, but there were sounds coming from the shop. Kate set down her parasol and handbag, then walked through to the cavernous space, happy to see the windows all open and fresh air blowing in steadily. After stepping over the barrel of a disassembled can-non, then navigating some packing crates (careful not to snag her skirt), she was able to examine some of the workbenches: tools of all kinds, clock mechanisms, various springs, several pistols in pieces, assorted daggers, dozens of measuring devices for size, weight, and volume, camera lenses and housings ... it went on and on, and these were just the small parts out being worked with. Kate knew there were large cabinets full of completed inventions, weapons, and ordnance. Jack was evidently preparing a strongbox for Kate to take on the journey, wiping it down with a rag.

"Did you speak to the authorities?" Kate asked.

"Yes. There's a regiment of dragoons combing the area. They're usually called out by the Excise officials when smugglers are about, so they know how to search."

"I hope they find and question those men. I still believe they may just be wealthy yeomen. Now that I think about it, running from them was quite a little adventure, even if they were farmers. Who do you think they are?"

"Frenchmen, maybe. Pam has a deep distrust of the French."

"Truly? The French?"

"Yes."

"Do you know why?"

"No."

"Oh." Kate was left entirely dissatisfied with her brother's answers.

"I've got this chest for you to fill," Jack said, as though the morning's events weren't worth further discussion. "Here's the missive for Tattersall." He placed a large waxed cloth envelope on the workbench.

"Yes, all right. Let me pack it. You can work on other things."

"Very good. Come and look at this." Jack strode to a carriage, one of several, and climbed up behind the splatter-board. "See?" He pulled a steering tiller back and forth, the front wheels responding smoothly. "My carriage should be easy to control. Not like other locomotion monsters that have crashed. The brakes and steering are essential."

"Is this the same carriage I drove on my last visit? You've painted it green?"

"Yes. I've added your improvements. And I believe I can get greater power from the engine just by adjusting the valves, forcing the steam into tighter passages."

He sat on the bench of his machine while Kate stood with her arms crossed inspecting his work. It had the same care and craftsmanship Jack put into his weapons. All the iron parts and large wooden surfaces were coated with a thick glossy layer of deep green, the heavy woodwork was oiled dark and polished to a shine, and the brass used for control wheels, handles, hubs, and other fittings sparkled. She had driven this carriage a few times over the last couple years, and felt happy to see her brother making use of her suggestions, but maintained a critical eye.

"When are you adding the battering ram?" This feature wasn't Kate's idea, but she had seen it in his drawings, and supposed it must be for knocking down old cottages or something. "Jack? Are you listening to me?"

He muttered while climbing down, and Kate thought it sounded something like "buttered rum." She suddenly looked at the carriage in a new light.

"Was it Palmerston who wanted the battering ram on there? Are you building this for him?" *Well, of course. He said he's building everything for him. Why a battering ram? Would it be for breaching walls? Or gaining entry to locked doors? I thought he was building these for everybody.* "Jack, don't you intend to sell these machines to everyone?"

"Everyone. Yes, yes," Jack murmured while studying some engine parts. These parts were always shipped covered in grease, so Kate stayed far from them, knowing a mere brush would ruin her outfit. She watched her brother smear the muck on his smock and cringed. Turning away, she checked her gloves and sleeves, lest she had been careless and soiled her clothing; happily she found them clean, and looked at the carriages, all in various states of construction.

"I'd like to have a steam locomotive carriage to drive hither and yon, through the streets of old London town. Or even better — what you need to build is a steam-propelled horse."

Kate spoke loudly, trying to get his attention. "I told you, people don't want to be confined to a carriage. They'll desire the ability to go anywhere a horse can, and at a gallop." She thought about the dragoons searching for the men from the valley. "There could be military applications. Think of the cavalry. Or a despatch rider."

"Yes," Jack said, putting his spectacles in place. "Yes, indeed. I have been working on that."

He led her to a workbench and sifted through several drawings before handing one over. Kate noticed problems immediately. Her brother was designing a thin carriage.

"This isn't what I meant," she said softly, trying not to hurt his feelings. Kate strode to the back of the workshop and peered about. She knew somewhere an old broken dandy horse lay stashed among the parts piles. Wheels, harnesses, carts, tools, pulleys, ropes, boilers, tarpaulins, crates, parts of guns, and countless indescribable bits of every shape and description lay before her in the half light. "There." She pointed to the contraption. "You should make it something like that."

"Oh?" Jack picked his way through the cobwebs. He took up the foot-propelled two-wheeled wooden vehicle and straddled it, rolling a little bit; the rusted wheels groaned. "Now I see what you mean."

He dragged it over to a workbench, Kate trailing.

"Jack, I've been thinking. Perhaps I should take a pistol with me on this voyage? For protection? I could at least scare someone with it."

"You know where they are. The weapons you fired today are all in the closest armoire."

Kate stepped to the cabinet and opened the doors. The mouldy smell from the oiled leather overpowered her lavender water. Wrinkling her nose to suppress a sneeze, she selected one of the newest pistols, with a belt, a holster, and a box of ammunition. She moved on to the rifle.

"I'm taking the nasty gun that hurts my shoulder," she called, then was startled to find Jack appear abruptly at her elbow.

"Yes, that's the one you need to deliver to Henry Tattersall. I've prepared four dozen cartridges for you." He started taking items off the shelves. "And here is a pair of my dust spectacles. They secure with a strap, the padding is soft around your eyes, and the yellowed lenses will filter sunlight."

"Similar to cinder goggles?" Kate thought of the engineers and firemen on the railways with their lenses, protecting their eyes from sparks and smoke.

"Except the tinted glass," Jack said, nodding, "and I use very soft leather for the padding."

Kate glanced over the items. "These goggles won't do anything for my looks, but if they protect my eyes they're worth having." She drew the pistol and tested it for weight and balance. "This is lovely, or whatever word I should use to describe a weapon. Jack, I'm very proud of you, making these for Foreign Affairs. Is Father aware?"

"No. I told you. It's a secret."

"But he's seen your inventions, and feels you're wasting your time. If you told him, think how impressed he would be?"

"Maybe some day. For now, don't tell anyone. Are you going to take that pistol?"

"I'd like to. I don't know how to carry it."

"You'll work it out."

Kate walked into the office and shut the door. By drawing up her skirt and petticoats, she managed to fasten the belt low around her waist, so the leather lay against her chemise and wouldn't rub on skin. She smoothed her clothing, the weapon completely hidden, hanging against her thigh. Feeling for the handle, Kate determined all she needed to do was sew a slit into a pleat, cut openings in the petticoats, and she would have access to the pistol. Waltzing about the office, letting her skirt sway, getting a feel for wearing the belt and holster, she felt suddenly more confident.

This is why people carry guns; it makes you feel safe. Kate took it off. *I could just stow it in my handbag, that would be easier.*

Moving back into the shop, she put the weapons in the strong-box. On the next bench over sat a wooden and brass camera, Jack's version of Daguerre's photograph-taking device. Kate realized it was a model she hadn't seen before.

"Is this the smallest you've built?" she asked, but Jack didn't answer, apparently fixated on his motor-propelled-horse drawing.

"Jack, may I take this on my tour?"

"Hmm? Yes, certainly. That one uses six-inch plates. Still silver on copper, but I'm working on an improved chemical process. I can't manage as good images as you make."

"It's probably the developing steps you have trouble with." Kate squinted through the viewing aperture.

She knew the real trick was in how the plates were handled before and after exposure. They needed to be slipped out of the device and into prepared envelopes until washed in a special solution, or they turned completely black. Kate had previously made several images of her niece and nephew, one of Phoebe doing needlepoint, and one of Jack at his desk.

"You have to properly care for the plates. You're too rough on them and don't follow your own instructions. Are Foreign Affairs operatives using these?" She looked up from the lens and found herself quite alone, suspecting the inventor had disappeared on one of his errands.

HASTINGS TO ROSETTA

The next morning, Jack, Phoebe, and their children came to the dock with Kate and Mrs. Farewell to see them safely loaded. The older woman, though inexperienced with travel, approached everything with a no-nonsense attitude, and Kate felt glad to have her take charge. In truth, if she had travelled with her brother, Kate would have had more to look after because of his constant distractions. As they stood on the dock, men laboured around them, loading and unloading long rowboats. The groans of the ship's timbers straining against their anchor chains, caused by the swells of the tide, were audible across the water despite the relatively calm sea. A cool breeze blew from the west, the sky was a forbidding grey, and the ocean appeared eerily dark; Kate couldn't determine if she was trembling because of a chill, excitement, or apprehension. Suddenly an officer in dark blue with brass buttons directed them to embark, so it was just quick hugs and kisses. Their chests and other baggage were collected by a crew, then the women had to edge down a steep plank from the dock onto a steam-powered ferry that took them to their ship. The fear of falling into the ocean struck Kate for a moment, but she brushed it aside and stepped along carefully but confidently. The ferry was quite new, shiny black with gold trim, the propeller hidden below the water. Black smoke billowed from the chimney, and Kate feared sparks might land on her new light yellow coat. The sailors were very helpful, knuckling their brows to the ladies, all smiles, and looking for the chance to aid Kate in any way possible. She nodded to the men, noticing their squinted eyes, deep tans, gnarled limbs, and calloused bare feet, judged them a rough gang, and made sure none had occasion to touch her, until an officer offered his hand to help her aboard the ship.

"I'm glad you're with me, Nanny," Kate said as they strolled around the deck. "In Portsmouth we'll find the finest inn available, then sail for Egypt. I cannot wait to go up the Nile!"

"Where Sir Thomas Roberts will be waiting for us?"

"Yes, on the other side, at Port Suez. He'll take us through to China. Do you know my grandfather quite well?"

"No. He's always been one to come and go. A great deal of old soldiers are so. Can't settle."

"I hope to talk to him about my mother."

"Don't get your hopes up. He was away on campaign in India and Spain most of her growing years. She married your father before he ever came back from the wars."

Kate thought about her grandfather for a moment. After their few visits, all she knew was he'd been a career soldier, made a fortune in India, and retired as a decorated hero after Waterloo. He was her only surviving relation on her mother's side, and she suddenly wished to know him better. *This will be an excellent opportunity for us to talk. He may not know much about my mother's childhood, but he can certainly tell me more about his life.* It was fortunate they had been able to contact him in Bombay and arrange the meeting.

"At least he's the ideal man to show us India and China. Isn't it exciting?" Kate exclaimed.

"I don't know if I'd use that word," Mrs. Farewell stated flatly.

❖

As they sailed from Portsmouth near the end of May, it was still cool on the ocean and rained frequently, horizontal biting drizzle that collected on the ropes and sails then whipped across Kate's face as she tried to walk along from mast to mast where the rolling of the deck was least noticeable. She wasn't certain which feeling was more uncomfortable: sitting in her cabin with a churning stomach listening to the ship creak while trying to make entries in her diary, or being soaked through from her less than dignified scrambles, where she could get fresh air and see the horizon. Every time the sails came around, tacking to catch the wind, the deck would pitch, and she had stumbled a few times. Meanwhile, Mrs. Farewell roosted in her berth, sipping tea. By the time the ship rounded Gibraltar and entered the Mediterranean Sea, the long sunny days were growing hot and windy, and the ship made great progress. The other wealthy people emerged to take the air. The ocean smelt different in the southerly climate, more salty, and the underlying hint of kelp was missing. Having travelled a bit before, Kate settled in and enjoyed chatting with first-class passengers. As they slipped past the sun-baked shores, with the constant sound of the wind straining the sails and water whirling past, she asked about places people had seen and their experiences. She had hoped there would be other girls her age on board, to perhaps cultivate friendships and share the journey, but everyone was older. Making brief stops off of Malta and Greece they picked up more passengers, so there were new faces to meet and ask about their travels.

During society training her stepmother had insisted that Kate maintain the sophisticated false face all the time, an aloof emotionless gaze. This hooded her eyes and kept her straight white teeth in reserve, only showing them occasionally to noble gentlemen who earned a lovely bright smile by being particularly charming. However, the freedom of the open ocean and the casual attitude on the ship soon had her grinning wide-eyed at everyone. She was invited to dine with the captain and his officers several times, but politely declined, feeling shy of the strong young men in their uniforms. After a few days, Kate had noticed the excitement of a sea voyage was wasted on Mrs. Farewell, but she appeared pleased with her cabin and the food.

"I can see you're happy to have made this journey," she said to the older woman as they finally sailed into port at Rosetta, having passed Alexandria earlier that morning.

"I'll admit, there is a curious appeal to it, but I'm not comfortable around all these foreign people."

"You'll adjust," Kate said, hooking her elbow so they could stroll along the deck together, parasols held high. She stayed quiet, considering Mrs. Farewell's unease. The ship carried mostly British, with a handful of French and Egyptians. She doubted her own words. *I wonder how she'll feel as we move farther into the Orient?*

"I've had interesting conversations with some of the foreigners on board," Kate said, trying to sound casual. "They are all decent people, really. Look, here's Mr. Bouguereau. He's an artist. I'll introduce you." She led the way to a neatly dressed, pleasant-looking man of about twenty-five leaning on the rail, staring out at the shore.

"Bonjour, monsieur." Kate collapsed her parasol and stepped close. "This is my travelling companion, Mrs. Farewell. She doesn't speak French, so please, if you don't mind, may we talk for a moment in English?"

"Yes, of course, my pleasure." He smiled and bowed to the ladies, then in a mock whisper said, "You must convince Mademoiselle Beaufort to pose for me when we put ashore."

Mrs. Farewell seemed startled by his request, but smiled in return. "She may listen to me on some accounts, but once she's made up her mind I can't change it."

"Yes, a headstrong young lady."

"Why wouldn't you pose for him, child?"

"He wants me to sit in the surf, completely naked!" Kate said laughing, knowing the shock her old nanny would have at such a thought.

"Pish! You scoundrel." Mrs. Farewell rounded on the artist, but didn't actually appear angry. "You Frenchmen are a saucy lot. You'll have a hard time finding a girl to do that."

"Mais oui." Bouguereau grinned. "If not mademoiselle, perhaps you would do me the honour?"

"Oh goodness!" Mrs. Farewell declared. "That would have to
be titled *Sea Monster* or something."

They all laughed.

"Now, you will excuse me, ladies." He bowed again. "I must
see to my baggage."

He wandered off and went below deck. Kate noticed Mrs.
Farewell was blushing.

"You see?" she prompted. "A very charming Frenchman."

"Yes, all right. Perhaps I can give more foreigners a chance,
as long as they speak English."

"Excellent. And I can always translate for you."

They watched as the sailors climbed the rigging and furled
the sheets of canvas into neat bundles, the officers calling orders
as the ship edged up to a sandbar. Without a breeze caused by
the forward momentum of the sails there was an immediate
change in atmosphere, the sun oppressive, the air hard to
breathe. Foul smells began creeping up around them, the dis-
tinct sour odour of unwashed sailors.

"It's starting to get uncomfortably warm," Mrs. Farewell
said while dabbing her forehead with a handkerchief. "I hope it
doesn't get any hotter."

Kate laughed, but couldn't help noticing the heat as well.
"I bought you a very light muslin dress to wear. Or you could
get by with just a skirt and shirt."

"You're not going out in just a shirt. What would people say?"

"I might. I'll wait until we're through Cairo. Then we'll be away
from our society. It's an option for when we cross the desert.
Or what about these robes I see the Egyptians wearing?" Kate
pointed with her parasol at the people on shore.

"You'll not go native, child. What do you mean, away from our
society?" Mrs. Farewell clenched her jaw. "What desert crossing?"

"From Cairo to Port Suez we travel by caravan. We're taking the new route established by that Waghorn fellow for the Egyptian Transit Company. It allows mail to come from India to England all year round in just six weeks!"

Mrs. Farewell glared with narrowed eyes and a frown. Despite being half a foot taller than Mrs. Farewell, Kate felt like a little girl who'd been caught stealing from the pantry. She tried her most winning smile.

"Don't grin at me, child. Caravan?"

"Ah, yes. Camels ..."

ROSETTA TO SUEZ

The ship was soon pulled up to the dock on the rising tide with enormous hawsers. Kate would have been thrilled to stay in Rosetta and explore, but she didn't want to put Mrs. Farewell out. Besides, they had a schedule to keep. As it was, because of the winds, they were already expecting to reach Suez a couple days late for their rendezvous with Kate's grandfather. They disembarked from the ship, Mrs. Farewell ensuring their baggage was safe while Kate stood staring at the nearby market. She stamped her boots in the dirt, grinning to herself, and did a little hop for joy. *Now the real adventures start — I'm in Egypt!* She thought about her atlas. *We're east of Constantinople. This is where the Orient begins!*

The city was all low buildings, except for an occasional dome or tall thin tower painted white, which she knew indicated where the Persian or Turkish churches were, although the proper names eluded her. She didn't know much about these other religions, and believed their followers were all being converted to Christianity. Some of the structures were stone, but the majority appeared to be crafted of brick, mostly plastered, a few painted with bright colours. She desperately wanted to do some shopping, and spotted many of the other passengers doing so, then saw Mr. Bouguereau give her a wave before disappearing into the crowds with a valise and easel. To call out a goodbye would have been wasted, drowned out by the birds and singing of the natives toiling around her.

The labourers, dark-skinned men in loose robes, with sandals or bare feet and various styles of coloured cloth head wraps, worked at a frantic pace, loading the bags, chests, and crates onto donkeys, which were then herded out of view in a cloud of dust. Kate glanced over her light grey travelling suit, decided it would probably be ruined by the time they reached India, and worried about when they were going to have the services of a laundry. In the distance she could see ladies in vividly coloured, enormously belled promenade gowns, covered in adornments, strolling along under palm trees on a grassy peninsula. They made her feel quite plain, but she judged the small profile of her outfit far more suitable for her purposes, and preferred travelling suits and riding habits over all her dresses anyway.

A ship's officer showed them and some of the other first-class passengers to a coach pulled by a weary-looking pair of horses, which conveyed them through the city to the Nile. The pungent smell of manure hung over the road, except where it passed by one area rich with cinnamon and other spices. Upon arriving at the Nile, Kate was surprised to find it appeared to be dammed, with only a canal going out to the sea. The water was extremely low and muddy. The men with the donkeys were there, already unloading.

A large boat, painted a blinding white, perhaps one hundred and twenty feet long, with a half-submerged paddlewheel near the middle of the side, sat waiting for passengers and baggage. The cabin filled almost the entire deck and rose up two levels, with the pilot's wheelhouse on top. There were open areas filled with tables and chairs, wide walkways shaded by canvas awnings, and row upon row of portholes. Smoke rose steadily from the pair of tall flues and steam blew off through the whistle every few minutes, so it was obviously ready to set out.

"This craft could never leave the safety of inland waters," Kate observed. "I don't believe it would hold up against our English rivers, not the way they have it."

"No," Mrs. Farewell agreed. "It's definitely built for the calm. And no rain. Anyway, it looks comfortable, let's get on."

Kate followed Mrs. Farewell up the gangplank onto a covered deck of polished wood. They were greeted by a boy in a red fez and white jacket with brass buttons, holding a tray of tall glasses containing a yellow beverage.

"This is welcome," Kate observed, taking a sip, trying to determine what kind of juice it could be. "They certainly hurry us along, don't they?"

"Indeed, child," Mrs. Farewell said, downing her drink and mopping her face with a handkerchief. "I hope once we get moving there's a good wind. I'm going to find a chair near the bow."

"All right, I'll join you presently. I want to look around the ship first."

Kate strolled to the starboard paddlewheel and tried to determine the construction. She estimated a forty-foot diameter, and imagined that with both wheels turning they might make six or seven knots, if the engines provided at least three hundred horsepower. These considerations came to her from years of working with her brother on his machines. Jack voiced clear opinions against paddlewheelers and felt rear screw propellers were a far more efficient and powerful way to produce thrust. She'd just climbed up an elaborate staircase to the front of the cabin's second level when there were shouts and the gangplank was pulled in.

Within minutes, the paddlewheels churning away creating a rhythm through the deck, Kate could see mansions and citrus groves spreading out from the city. Beyond the trees were wide green plains being harvested by hundreds of labourers. Indeed, it appeared idyllic, and worth spending some time visiting during their return voyage. She could understand why so many of the passengers they had travelled with from England were staying there.

Glancing around, perceiving no one nearby, she removed her lace gloves and unbuttoned her jacket, letting the breeze dry the

perspiration from her shirt and chemise. The front of her skirt
and petticoat were just high enough, a couple inches off the deck,
to allow some fresh air to blow on her legs. She felt sorry for
Mrs. Farewell, who she knew always wore long drawers, and the
gentlemen in all their layers and trousers. Kate was certain wearing
a single robe like the Egyptians would be far more practical. Male
voices speaking Spanish brought her from such thoughts. She
quickly did up her jacket, pulled on her gloves, and went in search
of Mrs. Farewell.

Soon they were passing abandoned buildings, with the plaster
falling off and caved-in roofs, where people seemed to take the
old bricks and build new homes. As the boat progressed out of
the Nile delta area there was much less cultivated land. Kate
couldn't imagine how a great nation had once existed here, with
only a small band of vegetation along the water, then miles of
brown stone and sand stretching as far as the eye could see.
The river was wide and winding, with dozens of steamboats
moving north and south, and countless little crafts appearing
in every patch of weeds along the shore; some looked to be
made of bundled reeds. There were also sailboats of various
sizes working their way up and down the Nile, tacking back and
forth to catch the wind, some of them European-style yachts
with high sides, cabins, and painted woodwork, others low and
flat with one very tall triangular sail, obviously favoured by the
natives. The erratic movements of the sailboats caused some
confusion as to who was steering where, and Kate speculated
on how often there was a collision, but felt entirely safe on the
large paddlewheeler.

A gong rang for dinner, so Kate and Mrs. Farewell reluctantly
left their breezy seats and found a table with the first-class
passengers. It was nice to eat in a dining room, with tables
and chairs of glossy dark wood, waited on by cheerful Egyptian
boys possessing toothy grins. They sat with a group of older
German people, who seemed determined to discuss business,

so while Kate understood their conversation about shipping costs and bad weather concerns, she stayed quiet and enjoyed the lamb and rice in cream sauce, washed down with more of the unnamed sweet juice and a glass of red wine. However, when she rose from the table to retire, Kate did ask to be excused in German, causing surprised expressions, which amused her greatly.

There was some confusion about cabins. Kate didn't have her lady's maid with her, but did have Mrs. Farewell, who was using Jack's passage, and the boat was segregated: single men down a particular hallway, single woman down another, couples and families in larger cabins near the bow, servants in communal rooms below decks.

"This will not do," a cabin boy whispered, and looked close to tears when he realized the mistake. "Please be letting me see what I can work out. I will find a steward."

"Very good." Mrs. Farewell nodded.

"We'll wait in my cabin," Kate suggested, and they entered while the boy ran off.

"This is very nice," Mrs. Farewell observed, running her hand over the sleek wood of the berth and looking at the embroidered carpet. "Much nicer than the ship."

"Yes," Kate agreed, noticing pitchers of hot water, basins, and cloths laid out on a toiletry table. "Ocean-going vessels seem to be more spartan, probably because of the conditions they have to sail through. This boat is like a floating inn. And I want you to have a first-class cabin, not a room with the servants. Do you mind if I take off some layers?"

"No, child, of course not. I'll stay proper until they find where I'm staying."

"I suppose we could share, but the berth is a little small, especially in this heat."

"Good lord! We haven't slept together since you were just a slip of a girl. I'd stretch out on the floor instead."

"Actually, now that you suggest it, we both could, Nanny.

Spread out the sheets and pillows, imagine we're bivouacking under canvas, in the wilderness. It would be fun!"

"Let's see what the cabin boy can arrange first. I confess, my spine would prefer a mattress, and a girl of your rank should have her privacy."

"Yes, all right," Kate said quietly, a little deflated. "I'm disappointed we didn't see any ancient monuments yet." She started unlacing her boots.

"Are we supposed to?"

"Yes, this is the land of the great pyramids. I've seen drawings of statues and temples. We'll probably pass hundreds in the night."

At that moment there was a tap at the door. Mrs. Farewell opened it to find the cabin boy all smiles again.

"I have room for you, ma'am. I move baggage. This way, please."

"Wait." Kate stopped him and handed over a penny. "Thank you," she said, smiling at him.

"Ah, thank you, miss," he exclaimed.

Kate then peeked out the door as they walked to the end of the hall. Once she saw Mrs. Farewell step into her cabin and the boy skip away, Kate quickly placed her boots just outside her door then eased it shut and secured the lock. She happily stripped down to nothing, made use of the chamber pot, and washed off with a soft cloth. She brushed her teeth and hair, extinguished the lamps, and stretched out on the crisp white linen, deliciously cool air blowing across her bare skin from the porthole.

Kate slept later than she'd intended, as she wanted to be on deck to see the sights. She dressed in her dusty light grey suit again, but with fresh chemise and hose, collected her cleaned and polished boots from the hall, did long plaits off her temples, then tied all her hair back loosely with a ribbon. Going up on deck she found the Nile completely flat, no waves to speak of, creating an ideal mirror of the landscape, then was shocked to see a man float by face down in the water. Other people were on deck, but they paid no heed. Kate swung away from the rail and shuddered, an odd tightness rolling across her scalp. She gasped and blinked, but the image of the man remained seared in her memory.

"Pardon me," she said to a passenger, an older man in a fine suit. "Is it common for the drowned to be left in the river?"

"He'll be picked up by someone, don't ye fear, dearie," he said with a Scottish accent and a reassuring nod. "We've lots o' victims in our rivers at home, too."

"Yes, I suppose we do," Kate agreed slowly, realizing the man was suggesting murder, and watched the body float out of sight. "Are you a frequent visitor to this land?"

"Aye, I live here."

"Then perhaps you could tell me, what is the name of the religion and churches here?"

"Muslim, and mosques."

"And the little towers have a special name?"

"Minarets. The muezzins call the people to prayer from there. You've probably heard their sing-song?"

"Yes, I think I have. I thought they were calling out the time, in place of clocks and bells."

"In some regards they do keep time. A Muslim's life revolves around prayer, five times a day."

"By gosh, the people are quite devoted to their faith."

"Aye, and the Copts, Egyptian Catholics, too."

"So someone shall give that man a decent burial?"

"I believe they will. Don't fret yourself, dearie."

"Thank you."

She entered the dining room, now feeling a little afraid of watching the river go by and perhaps seeing more dead, and remembered her father talking about the many bodies that were pulled from the Thames every day. Mrs. Farewell was already finishing a meal. Kate started with a cup of tea, relating what she had learned about religion, then selected a muffin. As her appetite returned, she enjoyed melon, oatmeal, and sausages.

About midday there was a noticeable shudder through the boat. Kate perceived the paddlewheels adjusting to a slower speed, then they turned towards a dock.

"Where are we?" she asked a passing crewman.

"Cairo."

"Really?" Kate spun around, scanning in all directions, seeing nothing but more low brown buildings with an occasional dome and minarets. "Where's the Sphinx? Where are the pyramids?"

"They're on the other side of the Nile." The man laughed and pointed west. "About an hour away."

"Oh? Pooh, I had hoped to see them from the river."

"You would have to take a ferry, then hire a coach on the other side. It's what all the wealthy visitors do. Now excuse me, miss, I must get back to work. We'll unload in a moment."

Mrs. Farewell approached with some documents.

"I've just been given these by a purser. They have a hotel for us on the far side of the city. It's quite new, built by the *P and O Company*, and the air is supposed to be fresher there. I hope that's true, I can smell the city already. The sooner we get through here the better. One of the carriages waiting by the dock is for us."

Kate stared across the Nile for a while, then resignedly turned to face the dock. She desperately wanted to see the great monuments, but there wasn't time. She consoled herself by thinking that perhaps on their return journey Mrs. Farewell might be more agreeable and there would be some days to linger in Egypt.

The odour reminded Kate of London when the cesspools overflowed, but that was always with heavy rains and wind washing the waste away quickly; here it was so dry, hot, and still. Air trapped between the buildings proved suffocating, the miasma causing uncontrollable gagging. Kate held a perfumed handkerchief to her face but could not escape the horrible sour salty taste. Thankfully, as they progressed through the city it opened up, the atmosphere grew less foul, and the wind found ways of blowing down the roads. They arrived at a three-storey hotel and found it quite luxurious, their rooms like a fine English establishment, but with a thin layer of dust on everything. By opening the shutters and leaning out the window Kate could see the desert stretching out to the east, nothing but sand and rock.

In the morning Kate pulled on her favourite knee-high buff leather boots, which tied at the ankles and buckled up the sides, and a beige silk riding habit. This suit had a long skirt, a waistcoat cut tight for bosom support, and a short jacket with some room in the shoulders to allow movement. She selected a broad-brimmed straw sun hat with light yellow and white veils, scooped up her frilly parasol, and thought with such an ensemble the desert shouldn't be too trying at all. She heard voices outside and looked out to see about thirty camels being guided to the space across from the hotel. Kate had seen and touched these tall, humped, long-legged animals during an exhibition held at the Zoological Gardens in Regent's Park, but the thought of riding the beasts made her quite excited.

After securing her various travel boxes, portmanteaus, and chests, Kate hurried down through the lobby and out into the scorching sunrise. They had been instructed to start as early as possible, then take a rest during the middle of the day. The handlers used a small stick to tap the animals on the backs of their legs, and they dutifully knelt down onto their shaggy stomachs, some bellowing while doing so. Immediately baggage started to be loaded. Marching across the road she determined some of the camels were for cargo — dirty, less-cared-for beasts — while others, cleaner and kitted for riding, were for passengers. Kate took a good look at one lying on bended knees before her. The rope bridle, decorated with coloured tufts of earthy red, green, and yellow, and the heavily padded saddle, constructed with tall front and rear pommels and secured by a girth strap, appeared similar to horse tack. The odour was entirely different. Kate liked stables and the sweet fragrance of hay, the lather a horse created when galloping, the wet leather saddle flaps, but the camels smelt strongly of urine and manure.

"Mrs. Farewell! Over here!" Kate called out to the woman when she saw her emerging from the dark lobby onto the dusty road.

"Good Lord, the heat! Oh my, these creatures smell awful. Horses are much more civilized."

"Yes, Nanny, I agree. I'll always ride a horse if I may. Did you have breakfast?"

"I did, and you?"

"I'm too keen to get started. I'll have something at the first stop. So ... are you ready to try?"

"Couldn't we take a carriage?"

"It's not an option. We have to make do with the camels. This is new to me as well."

"Fine for you," Mrs. Farewell snapped. "You're a natural-born rider. I remember your escapades. Racing all over hell's —"

"Mrs. Farewell!" Kate glanced around and was relived no one else seemed to be listening.

"You're quite certain there are no wagons to ride on? They tie our chests on these creatures?"

"There are the crates of Bibles moving off now," Kate said, pointing out two camels walking into the sunrise with a boy leading them. "If crates go by camel there must not be wagons."

The ladies watched a bejewelled man with a long beard, in silvery robes and matching turban, wearing spectacles with dark coloured lenses, climb easily onto the saddle of a beast. A handler gave a tug on the bridle, and it rose awkwardly with a cloud of dust. The man sat sideways on his hip, shifting on the cushions, placed one foot in a stirrup, then tapped the camel's shoulder with a stick and they lumbered off.

"That didn't look so bad," Mrs. Farewell admitted. "Let's get on with it then."

They approached a couple of the smaller mounts and tentatively poked the cushions. A dark man in a battered top hat and brightly striped robe, with a stack of papers tucked under one arm, appeared behind them.

"You are the Beaufort party, yes?" he asked, smiling, showing extraordinarily deep wrinkles and large yellow teeth.

"We are," Mrs. Farewell responded.

"I am Mr. Nafik, caravan master." He bowed grandly with a sweep of his free hand. "I shall see to all your needs. I have two ladies and a gentleman on my manifest."

"Ah, yes." Kate nodded. "The gentleman is not with us."

"As you say, of course. I will adjust the cost. Please begin your journey: we have far to go, and it will only get hotter."

Other than the jerk caused by the camel rearing to its feet, Kate made out quite well, shifting from hip to hip on the cushions, using the stirrups on and off for balance, holding her parasol, and searching the barren landscape for wild animals. The camels followed the handlers without much prodding, so the passengers didn't have to be concerned with controlling their mounts as they spread out, forming a long line into the desert. It seemed to be mile after mile of sand and rock, with an occasional pile of bleached bones, sun-blasted and desolate — the most inhospitable country Kate could imagine. She often glanced at Mrs. Farewell, and could see the poor woman was miserable, but suffering stoically. Once they reached Suez and put out to sea, Kate knew it would be considerably cooler. Also, they would be with her grandfather and a crew of retired British soldiers, so the older woman would feel more at home.

Within an hour of setting out they formed up with other parties until the caravan grew to about eighty camels, the passengers given positions near the front of the line, where less dust was kicked up. Rest breaks were frequent, and there were latrines available solely for the use of European women. The heat was like a furnace, and Kate found her perspiration instantly drawn away by the hot wind. They wore veils over their faces, but sand still invaded mouths and noses and stung their eyes. Mrs. Farewell tumbled from her camel the first time it knelt for a dismount, not hurting her, but obviously wounding her pride. Kate, hanging on tight as her camel knelt, bit her tongue not to laugh, and quickly helped dust the older woman off. On the trail they saw strings of donkeys, riders on horses, and wagons and carriages, some moving along quite quickly, causing Kate to feel like she'd let her old nanny down. Mrs. Farewell shrugged it off, however.

"I know this was booked ahead, and I'm here in place of the Viscount."

"Yes," Kate agreed. "But I really had no idea coach passage was an option. Jack planned all this through an agent. I'll ask Mr. Nafik about it when next we see him."

The first night with the caravan was spent in a hotel similar to the one they had just left, a little plainer and not quite as clean, with limited choices for supper but no shortage of fried spicy paste patties, flatbread, and sugared ginger. There was indeed room in a coach for Mrs. Farewell, so arrangements were made for her to make the rest of the journey with three Dutch women. Mr. Nafik required only a small amount to make the adjustment, which Kate gladly agreed to. The Egyptian was very attentive to all his customers, spoke excellent English, and always wore a smile. Most of the men and boys working the route appeared quite tough and taciturn, not friendly, dressed in dusty white robes and head wraps that could be adjusted to cover their faces. They seemed intent on business, were very efficient, and avoided all the ladies. However, Kate noticed some of them staring at her on a few occasions, watching while she smoothed her skirt or adjusted her unruly hair. She imagined they didn't interact with European women very often.

The second day Kate added her goggles, wearing them under her veil, and found them ideal, taking away the glare and providing protection from the wind-driven dust and sand. Other people on the caravan had similar eye protection, but Kate suspected hers were the best. She hadn't followed the string of camels very far when to the south several pyramids became visible. They weren't the enormous smooth-sided style she'd expected, but were still large, with stepped sides. There was nothing but scorched desert all around, and she couldn't imagine how the labourers could have survived such conditions.

That night, which became quite cool, Kate and Mrs. Farewell shared a large tent with tapestries, carpets, and embroidered pillows. Both of them were afraid that insects and snakes might skulk into their shelter, but upon inspection saw the sides and door flaps were exceedingly long, overlapped and folded under the carpets, creating a secure perimeter. It was the sort of bivouac Kate had suggested previously in the paddlewheeler, but genuine. She felt thrilled to be in such an exotic location, living like an Arabian, even if only in this small measure. She stayed up late under mellow lantern light, reclining on a nest of pillows, sketching in her diary and making notes about her experiences.

Although Kate thought she had grown marginally accustomed to the heat, when they reached Suez the prospect of getting out to sea was welcome. The brutal sun seemed to always be robbing her of breath and strength, her usually reliable limbs like noodles, and it caused dizzy spells and loss of appetite. As the caravan shambled down to the port she saw the usual little brown flat-roofed buildings, along with a large white mosque with four minarets. There were crowds at the docks loading and unloading the ships. It looked and sounded like a smaller version of Rosetta, but with a larger dock: labourers in loose robes and head wraps singing, birds circling overhead cawing. The sea, reflecting the perfect azure sky, stretched and widened to the south, a belt of green grew on the edges, then nothing but sun-parched hills of light brown.

The camel handlers led them into a rocky paddock where Mr. Nafik stood waiting. Kate climbed off her mount for the last time, lifted back her veil and slipped her goggles down around her neck, then stooped to peer into the camel's brown eye. It looked back calmly, barely moving. She didn't know if the beast had a name, and wondered how long it would live in these harsh conditions. *You're a tougher animal than me, to be sure. Good luck, little camel. Perhaps I'll see you on my return trip.* She rose, signed a receipt for Mr. Nafik, then followed the porters carrying her chests, bags, and the crates of Bibles down to a shipping station by the docks. A moment later Mrs. Farewell climbed out of a carriage and joined her.

Kate scanned the crowds for her grandfather. Before her churned a throng of incredibly varied people, the labourers mixing with ship crewmen, officers, and passengers of every description speaking different tongues, creating a confusing cacophony. Some travellers were in rough work clothes, others in decent suits and dresses, and then her class, wearing the finest silk fashions. In a few moments Kate glimpsed her grandfather working through the crowd, his height providing an advantage: he swivelled his head left and right as he approached. He wore a closely tailored white linen suit and black peaked cap. The old soldier appeared thinner than she remembered, long of limbs and body, as though a man with an already lean build had been stretched a foot too tall. His gaunt face and protruding cheekbones created an almost skeletal visage, but he had a spry step, remarkable for a man of about seventy years of age, and a twinkle in his large smiling eyes.

"Mrs. Farewell, hello." He walked past Kate without even a nod. "You must have come instead of Jack? I puzzled over who would accompany Kat. Whithersoever is she?"

"Grandfather! I'm right here!"

He spun on his heel and stood still for a moment, a look of shock upon his face, then smiled. "Kat, I ... I guess I expected a little girl dressed like a boy. My word, you look just like your mother." He removed his cap and bowed, white wispy hair sticking straight up, then stepped up to give her a hug.

"I'm so happy to see you." Kate tipped back her head and stretched up on her toes to give him a quick kiss on the cheek, then whispered, "I'm Kate, now. I haven't been Kat for a couple of years."

"Very good," he said softly. "I'm sorry it's been so long. I cannot believe how much you've changed. How old are you now?"

"Fifteen, but I stood this tall at thirteen. I think I'm done growing."

"I believe your mother was the same way. Quite mature at fifteen. She married your father two years later. How is he?"

"He's well. And my stepmother, too. Both very happy together."

"Good."

"How did you know Jack wasn't coming? Did everyone know but me?"

"You didn't know? I received a letter about a month ago."

"How have you been, Sir Thomas?" Mrs. Farewell asked.

"Fine, fine. You can call me Sir Tom. Let's collect your baggage."

Kate watched her grandfather take control of the situation. As a retired general officer it seemed only natural for him to direct the movements of the crates and chests. A barrel-chested man with extravagant whiskers waited on the dock with a group of old sailors, all wearing broad-brimmed straw hats, cotton shirts, and baggy sailcloth trousers.

"Do you remember Colonel Bob?" Sir Tom asked.

Kate examined the large grinning man for a moment. He was familiar, someone she'd met as a child. She seemed to remember something about him campaigning with her grandfather through India, Portugal, and Spain.

A Scotsman? Who never married? The one who ... "Yes!" Kate said, putting her fists on her hips and taking on a disapproving tone. "Colonel Murray. You're the one who uses foul language all the time."

"Bloody 'ell, she only thinks of that?" Murray looked around with his mouth agape and raised his eyebrows at the crew, who all enjoyed a good laugh.

Kate remembered her grandfather visiting and taking her sailing in the Bristol Channel when she was about nine years old. At the time he had adapted a sloop for his leisurely travel. Colonel Bob had been with him then, and Kate realized the boisterous man had frightened her. Watching him now, with his broad grin, she couldn't imagine why.

They loaded into a jolly boat, to be ferried out to the yacht. Kate was surprised when her grandfather pointed out a steamboat. The craft was about sixty feet long, painted red and black, with no sails, the only structures protruding from the deck a low cabin, a wheelhouse, and a chimney.

"When did you purchase a steam launch?" she asked as they approached the side.

"Four years ago," Sir Tom replied. "Glasgow-built. Her name's the *Otter*. She's an ocean-going vessel, but we avoid deep waters. I don't know how we'd manage in very rough seas, and without sails we can't afford to get too far from the coaling stations."

"Is the engine powerful?"

"Indeed. We stopped in Hastings after I took possession of her. Your brother rebuilt the engine and doubled our speed."

"Why didn't you visit us?" Kate felt a little hurt. "It's so like Jack not to mention it."

"We had to beat the stormy season around the Cape of Good Hope. We've been east of Africa ever since. Mostly India, and through to Burma. Out to China, too."

Once on deck, while Mrs. Farewell tended to their baggage with a couple of sailors, Kate explored a bit. The boat's ratter, a scruffy black terrier named Scrapper, followed her suspiciously, edging up to sniff at her skirt and jumping away if she turned to pet him. The cabin was built half above and half below the deck, so there were only three steps down to the hall leading to the galley, which took up the entire front half of the cabin. Off the hall was a navigator's office, a small armoury, the boat's tack room, and a salon with four chairs. From the galley another ladder led much deeper to the individual quarters, crew's quarters, the head (a chamber with a basin that dumped into the ocean and some rudimentary washing facilities), engine room, and storage. She calculated about twenty crew on board and every one of them quite old: men who had served as soldiers but were now content to be sailors. Kate and Mrs. Farewell would share quarters, a room fitted with four berths and a small porthole.

A while later, with lemon water in hand, they sat and chatted in the sunset, the sky, landscape, and sea turning a thousand shades of orange. Kate was happy to wash the dust from her throat, even if the beverage was warm. She looked across the bay at the quarantine station and pondered what poor souls might be languishing there. Shaking off such sad thoughts, she turned and examined Suez instead. The town stretched up from the water looking like mud bricks piled indiscriminately by a child. Some of the buildings that had appeared small from shore were in fact quite large, built along the steep rocky outcrops, going up three and four levels.

"Do we have time to stay here tomorrow?" Kate asked. "I would like to explore a market. We've been rushed thus far."

"You won't find much here," Sir Tom said, joining her at the rail with his pipe. "Everything is moving through the port to Europe, all packed tight for the journey, whether it's from India or China."

"Nothing gets shipped the other way?"

"Very little. Don't worry, there'll be lots of markets for you to waste your father's money in."

"Shall we stay in India long? Calcutta should be fascinating."

"On the way back from China."

"Why not on the way thither? Or both?" Kate suggested.

"My instructions were that you have an important missive and package to deliver to Canton. And to do so with alacrity," Sir Tom said firmly.

"I don't believe it. How do you know? Who gave you these instructions?" *This is bizarre.*

"I had orders from the Consulate's office in Cairo. They were waiting for me when I arrived at Suez."

"Orders? You're retired."

"I'm on half pay until I die, Kate. An officer never truly retires."

"May I ask from whom you received these orders?"

"Lord Russell."

"The Prime Minister?" Kate said, a little shocked. "Why would the head of our government be concerned about what I'm doing? It must be a mistake. Are you certain the orders are genuine?"

"Yes. Whatever it is you're carrying has to be delivered quickly and quietly."

"Grandfather, do you have any idea why? Or what this may be about?"

"No, but I suppose it has something to do with your brother. I believe he was originally tasked to carry out this delivery. Do you know what's in the package?"

"It has one of Jack's rifles."

"A rifle? I saw how large in size all your various baggage is. You don't have a rifle with you."

"Yes, I do. It breaks down into three pieces and fits inside a case. The barrel unscrews from the trigger housing. It's quite impressive. Jack told me it's for hunting."

"Why would delivering that be important enough for Russell to send me a note?"

"I have no idea." Kate thought a moment. "Maybe it's just the letter that's important? It's all for Foreign Affairs. I'm to capture images of all the new buildings being constructed by other nations at the Chinese ports as well."

"Foreign Affairs? So Palmerston ordered this?" Sir Tom demanded, his eyebrows knitting.

"Yes. You look angry, Grandfather. Is something wrong?"

"Palmerston was behind the war from 'forty to 'forty-two. A British army forced the opening of the ports. Thousands of Chinese were killed. It's what's led to all the problems there today."

"What problems?"

"The opium addictions. Millions of Chinese are dependant. The opening of the ports allowed smuggling to run wild."

"How dreadful. It's becoming a problem in England, too. Foreign Affairs is smuggling opium?"

"No, no. But it's their policies that allow it to happen."

"This is quite confusing," Kate said, more to herself than aloud. *Everything goes back to Palmerston and Foreign Affairs business ... taskings ... whatever. I wish I could remember exactly what he said to me. Anyway, it doesn't have anything to do with opium. I'm just making a delivery and taking some images.*

They sat silent for a few moments.

"Well, don't worry." Sir Tom grinned. "It doesn't affect you. We'll have a lovely voyage, and you'll get to see all the sights."

"Yes." Kate smiled, feeling lighter. "I'm so happy to be here with you."

"Good. And I'm delighted to have you and Mrs. Farewell. By the bye, who's receiving the deliveries?"

"The letter and package are both for a friend of Jack's, Dr. Tattersall." Kate felt a flutter inside thinking of him. "I'm ... I'm looking forward to visiting with him."

"Are you now?" He smiled and winked at her. "Do I hear a hint of affection in your voice?"

"Perhaps," Kate allowed.

With her stepmother or father she would have denied it vehemently, but somehow this man, whom she hardly knew, brought the truth from her. He stood quietly peering at her with large green eyes, and Kate perceived nothing but love and kindness behind them, no judgement or agenda.

"Promise me you won't tell anyone," Kate said quietly, feeling her face turn hot. "But I'd like to think of him as a prospective suitor."

"A man with no title? Aren't you at all concerned he might be a fortune seeker?"

"Oh no. If he pursued me I suppose that might be the case, but I don't know if he's ever given me any thought. And besides, his parents are gentry, wealthy landowners, wealthier than our family. The Tattersalls made thousands with horses."

"What kind of a man is he?"

"Absolutely brilliant!" *And strikingly handsome, with a strong chin and white teeth.* "He studied at Saint George's and received his diploma from the Royal College of Physicians at eighteen. He could be president of the Royal Society someday. He's able to recall everything he sees or reads, at least that's what Jack said."

"Oh, well, marry a man for his brains and you'll never be wanting for intelligent conversation, will you. How long have you known him?"

"I just met him in April. He sailed for China almost immediately. We had a few polite conversations about his work. Jack has known him for a few years through Royal Society functions and lectures, and vouches for his character."

"Did they attend university together?"

"Oh no, Jack went to Cambridge when I was an infant. Mr. Tattersall finished school a year ago. He's not yet twenty."

"So young? And bright. Do I dare guess he's a fine-looking lad?"

Kate didn't answer, just smiled and turned towards the sea, watching the gulls circle in the sunset.

"Very good ... sounds like he has a lot in common with my granddaughter. So, the delivery comes first, as Russell has ordered. I believe it's clear."

"Yes, I guess we do need to get to Canton as soon as possible."

"Indeed. We steam for China in the morning. Wait until you see the speed we can do!"

CHAPTER 8

SOMEWHERE OFF NAM KY

The *Otter* was remarkably fast, the shore passing by quickly, and they overtook other boats like they were standing still, leaving them far behind within minutes. They did travel through some rough seas, and poor Mrs. Farewell didn't fare very well. The long, thin shape of the boat caused some severe pitching, so the older lady stayed in her berth. Kate found it similar to when they'd sailed from Portsmouth, but her stomach didn't churn like it had previously. After a few days Mrs. Farewell's constitution adjusted, and she was able to help in the galley, enjoying the crew's company.

Summer was waning when they put into Singapore for coal, water, and provisions. Kate thought the city looked dirty and dangerous, refuse and rats visible on the docks. The quarantine station was flying a black flag, indicating bubonic plague, so she did not go ashore.

They were anchored one morning somewhere off Nam Ky, the peninsula between Burma and China, when Kate rose early to draw the coastline.

"Good morning," Sir Tom called, stepping along the rail to see her work.

"Good morning, Grandfather."

"Difficult to sketch once we're under way?"

"Yes, indeed." Kate nodded. "And this view isn't very interesting to draw. It's endless jungle. I wonder if tigers are in there?"

"Perhaps." He swivelled around. "Look, there's a junk off our port bow. Why don't you draw that?"

A square-sailed vessel, about forty feet long, approached them at speed. Kate peered at the odd boat and thought it would make a nice subject. She started adding it into her sketch while Sir Tom moved off towards the cabin. After a few moments of drawing the high, wide squared bow, low hull, and broad stern, examining her subject and trying to capture the shape of the craft, Kate noticed the junk was tacking in a decidedly aggressive manner, using the wind to draw near.

"Grandfather!" she called. "Doesn't that boat seem to be coming up on us?"

Sir Tom moved to the rail and took a long look. Kate strolled over beside him. On the junk, men were visible, filling the deck.

"Who are they, Grandfather?"

"Pirates," Sir Tom spat, then he turned and yelled, "Men! On deck! To me!"

"Really?" Kate looked at the junk again. "In that small boat? Don't pirates usually have warships, with cannons?"

"These aren't the buccaneers of old, Kate, sailing out of Port Royal. I'll wager most of them are poor, desperate men with nothing to lose."

"We can barely see them. How do you know they're pirates?"

"The only reason to have dozens of men massed on deck would be for a boarding party. Now get below."

"Men!" Colonel Bob appeared at the rail. "Prepare to repel boarders!"

"Can't we outrun them?" Kate asked, hoping for an escape. *This is wrong. There must be a way to avoid bloodshed.*

"Our steam's not up yet, we'll have to fight." Sir Tom looked out at the approaching boat. "They'll have to tack again before their attack run. We've time to arm ourselves properly. Men!" he bellowed. "Draw weapons from the stores!"

"Tell cook to hold breakfast!" Colonel Bob added, apparently more concerned with his morning meal.

The crew scurried, and orders were shouted all around, the

boat's ratter barking in alarm. Kate made for the ladder, jumped down the three steps into the hall, and rushed to the cabin the ladies were sharing. She found Mrs. Farewell dressing. Kate pounced on her strongbox, tripping on her skirt hem, and drew her pistol, hands shaking. *I can't believe I'm doing this. I don't know if I can use it. Could I actually shoot someone? Maybe I should give it to Grandfather.*

"What's all this?" Mrs. Farewell asked, clearly alarmed.

"We're being attacked by pirates," Kate gasped. "We have to defend ourselves."

"Yes, and take care of the men. There'll be wounded."

"Should we bolt ourselves in?" Kate suggested. "Yes, we'd be safer here."

"No! We have to help," Mrs. Farewell declared. "We need the men to stop the pirates on deck. If they get down here with us we'd be better off dead! Follow me."

When they emerged on deck, the crew were formed up in two ranks with Brown Bess muskets ready, Sir Tom and Colonel Bob with cutlasses at each end. Kate could see the men were calm, all of them professional soldiers who had fought in countless battles. She wished she could be so composed. Not entirely sure what to do, she stood behind and to the side of the men. She watched Mrs. Farewell stride up to her grandfather and say a few words. Various swords had been brought on deck in a barrel. Kate grabbed a long, thin sabre similar to the duelling blades she'd practised with as a youth. The junk tacked and drew near. Mrs. Farewell came back to her.

"What are you doing, Nanny?"

"Getting orders from Sir Tom. We'll hold the cabin door and look to the wounded," she declared. "The galley will be our hospital."

Mrs. Farewell put an arm around Kate's waist and guided her to the ladder. They eased down the steps into the hall and peeked out, their legs hidden below deck level. The junk approached from the starboard quarter side, allowing Kate to see it from her position. Now she discerned that the attackers' craft was very old and showing signs of damage, the woodwork lacking the required finishes and with pieces missing. The pirates were clearly visible, Asian men of various ages, some with long moustaches, drawing curved swords with large blades and placing their scabbards aside. She watched, holding pistol and sabre ready, trembling all over.

"Front rank prepare to fire!" Sir Tom bellowed.

Oh, my heart, it's going to leap right out of my breast.

"Our first volley will be into their sail. Perhaps we'll scare them off."

I hope that works.

"Front rank, aim!"

Please frighten them away!

"Front rank, fire!"

An ear-splitting roar of shots like a sharp clap of thunder rang out, and smoke filled the deck, obliterating all view of the pirates for a moment, then wind swept across the sea and the junk came closer.

"Front rank kneel. Reload. Second rank prepare to fire."

The deck of the junk was filled with men, mostly wearing ragged grey shirts, a mix of swords and daggers at the ready.

"Second rank, aim! Into the devils this time!"

Kate edged sideways to have a better view and bumped into Mrs. Farewell, who had fetched a cleaver from the galley.

"Second rank, fire!"

Again a thunderous roar and smoke.

"Second rank reload, front rank present!"

As the smoke cleared Kate tried to judge what effect the volley had inflicted on the pirates and could see none, the junk's rail still full of rough, yelling men waving their swords menacingly.

"Front rank, aim!"

The junk glided up, almost upon them.

"Front rank, fire!"

This time Kate saw men drop, as though their legs had simply folded under them, before smoke filled her view. Cries of pain and war sounded from the pirates. With a solid bump they came along-side the *Otter*.

"Fix bayonets!"

Kate backed a step down the hall with Mrs. Farewell, staring out amidships where the battle was poised to take place. The pirates started to swarm over the rails.

"Second rank, aim! Fire!"

Another roar and smoke, this time Kate watched aghast as men hit the deck, sprays of red mist filling the air.

My God, that's blood!

"Charge!"

The crew stormed forward, burying their bayonets into the lead-ing brigands. Clearly the trained soldiers were a far more effective fighting force, and the long reach of their weapons gave them a huge advantage, but there were so many of the enemy it was a desperate situation. Kate saw her grandfather hacking and slash-ing at the closest end of the skirmish. She watched, her pistol ready, trying to interpret a mix of emotions: encouraging excite-ment to revulsion and fear. Suddenly, Kate was terrified to observe a group of pirates boarding near the unguarded stern. The men came behind the line of sailors, directly for the cabin.

Oh no, what do I do? Somebody, help! There's no one! "Help!" she screamed.

"Get behind me!" Mrs. Farewell pushed Kate back.

The pirates reached the cabin door, and everything seemed to slow down for Kate. She knew she was yelling, but could hear nothing except an overwhelming rush of wind, like standing in a violent gale. She raised her pistol, aimed at the ladder, cocked the hammer, closed her eyes, and fired again and again, hoping her shots would force the men to retreat. When she blinked her eyes open, the hall was full of smoke, the strong sulphurous smell and taste of gunpowder choking her. The sounds of battle returned to her ears, but muted from the pistol blasts. She still cycled the hammer and trigger, but her rounds were spent. Stepping forward, she stumbled on Mrs. Farewell.

"Nanny! Nanny, are you all right?"

"Yes. I just dropped when you started shooting!"

Kate knelt over the woman, finding the air clearer lower down, holding her sabre out. Suddenly, a pirate appeared before them, his tattered grey robe and beige sash making him almost invisible in the smoke. He peered though the gloom, looking over them towards the galley, then charged forward, thrusting with his wickedly curved blade, running straight into Kate's sabre. A mix of shock, relief, and horror flashed through her upon seeing the point of her blade stab into the man's stomach. His forward momentum forced the sharp steel clean through his body. The pirate shook, then pitched forward onto his knees, coming face to face with Kate. Young and very thin, his large brown eyes were wide open, his chin trembling.

Oh no, help! I've killed him. No, please, no ... we're about the same age.

Kate realized he still clung to his sword and could easily strike at her. She let go of her sabre, leaving it sticking grotesquely out of his torso, climbed cautiously to her feet, then stooped over and pulled Mrs. Farewell away. The older woman struggled upright, and they both took a few steps back, holding each other. The smoke had mostly cleared. Kate couldn't take her eyes off the young man kneeling before her.

"Perhaps we can help you?" she said weakly, but suspected he couldn't understand and the wound would prove fatal. *I'm watching him die. It's my sabre sticking out of his body.*

The pirate gave a bit of a nod, closed his eyes, then fell over, letting out a low moan.

Kate turned to Mrs. Farewell and collapsed into her embrace. *My heart, my heart is ripping open.* She clung to the woman's shoulders and sensed tremors running through her body. Kate's knees turned weak, tears soaked her face, and she choked.

"I ... I cannot breathe." Kate didn't recognize her own voice, a shrill squeak. "I need air." She couldn't think straight, it felt like she might suffocate. Dashing for the ladder, ignoring Mrs. Farewell's cries to come to the galley, Kate leapt over the pirate and scrambled up into the daylight.

"Hurrah, hurrah!" The crew cheered their victory and yelled obscenities at the retreating attackers. The junk sailed away. Dead and wounded pirates lay bloody all along the deck. Kate was appalled to find dead men splayed out at her feet. Her grandfather approached, eyes wide.

"What are you doing on deck?" he demanded.

Kate barely recognized him. He looked wild, with blood splattered on his face and clothes.

"I'd say she helped defend the cabin from these goddamned brigands," Colonel Bob declared. "Good show!"

Kate glanced down at the dead again, then ran to the rail thinking she might vomit over the side, gasping and shaking. Upon turning back she was horrified to see the crew bayoneting the wounded pirates and tossing them overboard. The men were showing no mercy. The sky and sea reeled around her. She stumbled around the cabin and found open deck at the bow, where apparently no fighting had taken place. She was sitting down in a ball, leaning against the cabin, when Mrs. Farewell came to her.

"There now, child. Are you all right?"

"Nanny, I ..." *I have no words, it's all so horrible.* "Are you? All right?"

"Of course, but I must tend to the wounded. Can I leave you?"

"Yes, let me sit awhile." *I'm starting to see straight.*

"I could use your help, as soon as you're ready," Mrs. Farewell said. "Take some deep breaths, then join me in the galley."

"You ... you want me to help you?" *I don't know if I can.*

"Of course, and it's expected. You're a lady. You have to be strong, show a good example."

"Oh, oh dear, yes." *I must act composed, carry on no matter what.* "Yes, I'll do it."

They shuffled to the galley, Kate determined to be of some use and strengthened by seeing the deck and hall were clear of pirates. It allowed her to push the horrific scenes she had just witnessed from her mind.

Five wounded crewmen were in the galley. As old soldiers, the men were tending to the cuts, or even caring for themselves. They were rowdy, filled with the joy of their victory, and started singing campaign songs while downing rum.

"What the hell's going on here?" Colonel Bob appeared at the door. "I need two men stoking, sharp, we must get our steam up!"

"Aye-aye!" The uninjured men, except the cook, moved to get the *Otter* under way.

"I'll need basins of hot water," Mrs. Farewell said. "And clean cloths."

Kate hurried back and forth from the stove, bringing the basins and trading rinsed cloths for bloody ones. The wounded men continued to drink and sing. Kate admired their bravery, and she felt better.

"The men all need stitching," Mrs. Farewell judged. "These two first."

The cook brought out a surgeon's kit.

"Child, take a hooked needle and put some of that thread on it, then dangle it into the boiling water."

Kate did as she was told, racing to the stove and back. "Have you done this before?" she asked, astounded by the woman's calm and decisive actions.

"Yes, child, of course." She nodded.

"When? I thought you've never left England."

"That's true, but we have a long tradition of rioting, and of cavalry breaking those mobs. I've seen women and children trampled and cut down by sabres."

"Truly? Our own troops attacking the commoners?"

"Yes, but now's not the time to talk of that. Hand me the needle and prepare another."

Kate took a moment to clean up a bit while Mrs. Farewell stitched. *I hope the men are going to be all right. I think the wounds aren't too serious.* She thought of her thumb, and the time she split open a knee falling off a horse. *Yes, I've had similar injuries. I'm dealing with this quite well. As long as I don't think about the battle ... I mustn't think about the battle.* Getting the next needle ready, she noticed her dress was ruined, splattered with gore. *Oh no, is this the young pirate's blood? No, don't think about him. It must be from the injured crewmen ...* Everything had happened so fast she couldn't recall the action in detail. *I must concentrate on the wounded.* Kate felt a dull ache behind her eyes, a numbness setting in, and found herself stuck in place, holding a fresh basin and cloths.

"We need to bind this now." Mrs. Farewell, having finished the worst cut, looked at Kate.

"You've done a fine job," the old soldier said, glancing down at the stitching running from shoulder to nipple and taking another swig of rum.

"Bind it with what?" Kate asked.

"Silk would be best," Mrs. Farewell replied. "It breathes."

"I'll cut up this outfit. It's ruined anyway."

"Very good, child. Be quick."

Kate ran to her cabin and undressed. She wanted to wash, but there wasn't time. Pulling on a clean suit, she hurried back to the galley and started cutting strips.

"Go ahead and start binding," Mrs. Farewell ordered.

"How?"

"I'll do it," the cook declared, taking the bandages.

Kate was able to continue cutting and tearing, preparing needle and thread, fetching basins and rinsing cloths. *I'm managing. I could help in an infirmary.* Her hands started to feel chafed. *It would just take practice, and there are some skills to learn.*

When Mrs. Farewell started to work on the fifth man, the wounded were all quite drunk and singing merrily. Kate went on deck to get some air. A refreshing wind blew over her. The boat proceeded northeast at a good speed, the smoke from the chimney continuously streaming out and vanishing far behind. She guessed they would make haste for some time, lest any other pirates be lurking about. Sir Tom and Colonel Bob were standing over some long, lumpy bundles with several crewmen gathered around. The old soldiers were muttering softly, their heads down, faces looking sullen and tired. Drawing close, she slowed, realizing by the shape of the bundles it was three corpses being sewn into blankets. The boat's ratter lay on one man's chest, licking the blood that had soaked through the off-white material.

"A light butcher's bill," Sir Tom whispered to Kate, drawing close and guiding her towards the bow. "How are you?"

"Three of your men were killed?" Kate ignored his query.

"Yes, all old gunners. They went down fighting. They wouldn't have wanted it any other way."

"What will you do with them?"

"Bob will say a few words, then we'll put them over the side. There's coal and musket shot at their feet to take them down."

Kate started to weep; she wasn't sure exactly why. Too many thoughts went through her head. "If I had been killed, is that what you'd be doing to me? Sewing me into an old blanket to throw overboard?"

"Oh, hush now." Sir Tom hugged her. "Don't have such thoughts. I'm not going to let anyone harm you. Why don't you go below?"

"No. I want to attend the funeral. The men deserve that."

"Very well." He put an arm around her shoulders and eased her back amidships. "Let's get on with it, Bob."

"Bring them over to the rail," Colonel Bob instructed the crew. "And remove headdress."

The men pressed forward, as though helping to lift the bodies to the edge of the deck were important to them, acting like pall-bearers. Once they were standing reverently, with hats in hand, Colonel Bob continued.

"To every thing there is a season, and a time to every purpose under the heaven."

My heart aches. She started to sob.

"A time to be born, and a time to die; a time to plant, and a time to pluck up that which is planted."

Kate turned to Sir Tom and buried her face in his lapel. Her throat constricted. Colonel Bob's words drifted far away. She heard the men in the galley singing something low and slow.

I must be strong. I've got to watch this. She took a deep shuddering breath, then turned back to the funeral.

"We commit these our brothers to the deep, trusting they will rest in peace," Colonel Bob went on, "until the second coming, and great resurrection, when the sea gives up her dead and all rise for judgement. Amen."

"Amen," the men echoed together, then knelt as a group and carefully eased the corpses over the side. Kate stepped forward with Sir Tom to see the bundles rotate and fall into the water, the light colour of the blankets disappearing as they sank slowly into the dark waves and the *Otter* ploughed away through the sea.

"Oh." Kate let escape a tiny sound with a gasp.

The dog whimpered.

"Well said, Bob," Sir Tom said loudly so all could hear.

Many of the crew muttered agreement, or just nodded. They replaced their hats and started moving off to various duties. Kate glanced up at her grandfather and saw tears had streaked his face, running down inside his stiff collar. The ache behind her eyes suddenly seemed blinding.

"I'm going to lie down for a while," she whispered.

Sir Tom, eyes red-rimmed, his face like stone, nodded and let his arm drop from her shoulder. Kate walked unsteadily to her cabin, numb all over, climbed into her berth and lay, eyes closed tight, thinking of Quantock Hall, the hills and forests, her dog, and her favourite horse.

✛

Late in the afternoon, with rain blowing in, Kate realized she hadn't eaten all day. Her insides ached. She stood by the rail at the bow, staring at the dark clouds, wondering about the boy she had killed. His sad eyes haunted her, and the images of the bloody pirates strewn all about the deck pushed into her memory as well.

Sir Tom, in a fresh white shirt and tan trousers, smoking his pipe, appeared beside her.

"How are you, Kate?" he asked quietly.

"I don't know, Grandfather," Kate responded, still looking out at the ocean. "Do you think those pirates had wives? Children? How will they manage?"

"When they're coming at you, in the heat of battle, does it make a difference?"

"No, I suppose not. I had no choice, it was really an accident."

"Don't overthink things," he said, patting her shoulder. "We've all got to die sometime. No one knows when. You can have a long life hiding, or you can get out and live and take what comes."

"Dr. Tattersall said something just like that, when I asked him about the dangers of his work in China."

"There, he understands the risks and faces them. Death is all around us, all the time."

"How many men have you seen die?"

"Thousands."

"But you still get misty?" Kate recalled the funeral.

"I'm growing sentimental in my old age," Sir Tom admitted, with a bit of a smile. "Bob has a way of making me reflect on life."

"Indeed I do," Colonel Bob said. He stood directly behind them with a broad grin. "It's because I'm such an eloquent orator."

Kate and Sir Tom turned to face him. The man was still grimy and gore-splattered from the skirmish.

"Get cleaned up, Bob," Sir Tom said. "Make sure all the men do before dinner. We have ladies on board."

"Aye, all right." He nodded, then placed his heavy hands on Kate's shoulders, smiling and peering into her eyes. "So, how's our little soldier?"

"I'm not a soldier," Kate replied weakly.

"Well, you were as good as any recruit I've ever seen."

"Thank you, I guess." *Now please stop talking about it.*

"Your first kill!" Colonel Bob exclaimed. "I remember getting three in my first fight, and seven in the next."

"Oh, you don't keep count, do you?" Kate felt revulsion at the thought.

"Why, yes, I used to," Colonel Bob exclaimed, grinning. "Most soldiers do when they're young. Ha ha! After a dozen battles or so ... then you don't bother."

"My goodness." She considered the old campaigner with dismay. "How morbid."

SEPTEMBER 1849, CANTON

The young pirate came towards her, his sword thrusting, eyes dark and staring, always charging forward. She backed down the hall, but it never ended, and still he advanced, relentless, his blade at her throat. Kate screamed for help, but no sound came from her mouth, and then she was naked, utterly defenceless, the pirate coming through the smoke ...

Kate suffered from nightmares for more than a week, waking in a cold sweat shortly after going to sleep. She found solace in the company of the boat's ratter and started playing with the scrappy terrier, letting him curl up at the foot of her berth — after she gave his greasy fur a thorough scrubbing. However, despite her adoption of the dog, he would still playfully bite her skirt and bootlaces whenever Sir Tom said, "Attack the girl." This led to much amusement, Kate dodging and jumping around the deck while everyone laughed. It would usually end with her on a high refuge, Scrapper looking up and wagging his tail; then they could be friends again. Kate found the entire exercise pleasantly distracting, and inwardly knew it was an excuse to behave like a girl and be unladylike.

❖

In early September they turned into the Pearl River estuary. Dozens of boats moved about the vast waterway: tiny one-person crafts, sleek three-masted clippers, and enormous cargo ships.

"Is that Canton?" Kate asked, pointing out a city on the south bank, a grey stone fort and church visible.

"No, that's Macau," Sir Tom replied. "The Portuguese built it three or four hundred years ago. It's in a rough state, now. On one of the islands to the north is Victoria Town. It's the new English settlement."

Kate could see boats at anchor in the distance, with tall, steep green hills and mountains all around. They soon approached a narrows, and she feared there might be a collision. Large ships flew various national flags, fishing boats worked in pairs with broad nets, clumsy-looking junks and countless other little vessels all wallowed, tussled, or pushed for their part of the river. On the shore were nine ramparts, heavily fortified with hundreds of cannons, but they passed without hindrance. Kate saw natives toiling in the lush meadows under their broad round reed hats, immense hills behind them. The buildings along the bank were mostly small wooden structures, some built on piles out over the water, but then she spotted a lofty pagoda, the tall tower appearing to be a narrow pile of brightly decorated tents, magically suspended upright into the sky. She started to see large buildings of bluish brick, and every ten minutes more structures appeared, then a pair of huge, graceful-looking pagodas standing close to shore, the gold decorations glinting in the sun. Kate discerned a shift in their speed, the boat slowing, and upon walking to the bow she saw hundreds of small native crafts, then beyond them thousands, and on shore a low city with brown clay tile roofs stretching out into the distance, another pagoda to the north, dozens of brightly coloured box kites floating in the breeze, then more steep green hills and mountains.

Coming to a stop, it was noticeably hot and humid, but not as tropical as it had been when they were near the equator. A myriad of ships and boats of every size filled the water. The activity seemed chaotic and frenzied, making the docks in Egypt seem lazy in comparison. Kate watched endless lines of little crafts and barges ferrying between the storehouses and ships, or other destinations along the river. The majority of the boats were built like twelve-foot-long cradles, with a wicker covering at one end, and were propelled by a pair of girls or women, one pulling an oar at the bow, the other using a heavy scull off the stern. Many had little dogs on board and joss sticks burning, which created a sweet smoke hanging in the air. All the Chinese people seemed to be wearing baggy blue cotton shirts and trousers and had their hair done in long single braids. On both sides of the river were landings built with granite steps, where women were doing laundry. There was a constant murmur: the multitude of voices blending together, then the crackle of firecrackers, and a never-ending clamour of distant gongs at all different pitches and volumes.

They crawled up the river a little farther and Kate had a view of the European portion of Canton. First there appeared a very English-looking church of clean new stone with a square tower and tall heavy fences enclosing portions of the waterfront with trees inside. Poles as tall as ships' masts stood in a line about a hundred feet apart, flying various national flags, with impressive pillared two-storey buildings beyond. As the *Otter* was steam-powered, they were able to manoeuvre around the various sailboats to a mooring point. Colonel Bob ran the yacht up onto the mud beside some logs, near the church where trees were growing.

"May we visit Dr. Tattersall's infirmary today?" she asked Sir Tom.

"If the officials clear us, yes."

"Oh, Grandfather, I shan't sleep if we don't." She had already donned her gold outfit, plaited some of her hair, added ribbons, and applied a bit of cosmetics, knowing the combination created an adult semblance.

"Ho ho, cannot wait to see your young man?"

"Ah, well ..." Kate glanced around the deck to ensure no one stood in earshot. "He's not really my young man, although I do enjoy hearing you put it that way ... I would like to see him, and we have to deliver the letter and package."

"And we will, as soon as we're able. The first time we go ashore, bring the envelope, but leave the rifle behind."

"Why?"

"I'm little concerned about this arrangement," Sir Tom said with a frown. "It seems a trifle odd to me. Let us feel things out a bit. I'm certain you'll want to visit Tattersall more than once?"

"Yes, if he's not too busy, and is willing to see me."

"Very good ... and look, here comes a harbourmaster."

Only a skeleton crew stayed aboard the *Otter* while everyone else went ashore. Colonel Bob marched off to purchase supplies with most of the men. Sir Tom acted as guide for the ladies. Walking around the port, wide-eyed at the throngs of people who seemed to represent every nation, Kate felt quite safe seeing European and Chinese soldiers or police everywhere, standing guard and patrolling in small groups.

"I had no idea it would be like this," Mrs. Farewell declared, watching a party of women saunter past in what appeared to be bright Parisian fashion, escorted by Danish officers in dress uniforms.

"Nor I," Kate agreed. "I feel like we're in Europe."

They walked between iron railings that enclosed large parks, inside of which Europeans and Americans were taking leisurely strolls, made clear by their languages and accents. Kate peered around trying to spot a Chinese person other than the shabbily attired labourers. On closer inspection these men all had their heads shaved except the back, from which grew a long braid. Most wore blue, but there was some pink and lots of dirty white.

"I thought there would be elaborate temples," Kate said. "Beautiful yellow ladies in colourful embroidered robes, and fierce men with halberds and swords, wearing armour and capes, riding magnificent steeds."

"All you've seen are paintings of the ancient Chinese. It isn't like that here, we're in the foreign section of the city," Sir Tom said. "For over a century all shipping in or out of China was through this port, so the Europeans have become entrenched. Now there are five cities like this, but they all have restrictions as to where outsiders may work or visit. These are the Thirteen Factories," he said, indicating the buildings that dominated the waterfront.

The factories were side by side, facing the river, some with national flags flying in front. The imposing façades resembled English banking establishments, two storeys rising about thirty feet, with large stone pillars and enormous main doors, and anywhere from twenty to one hundred and twenty feet wide, stretching back farther than Kate could determine. The grand portion of the buildings existed only at the south ends, then they became a rather confusing collection of lower two-storey structures cobbled together with smaller entrances every twenty or thirty feet.

"Does each country make something different?" Kate asked.

"No, they don't make anything," Sir Tom explained. "They just receive goods and ship them. The word comes from 'factor,' like an accountant. They serve more as business markets. Each one contains many large clerks' offices with storerooms where examples of products are displayed. There are businessmen and their living quarters, shops, and some hotels. Most people who visit aren't like us, they're buyers come to secure boatloads of merchandise. The large warehouses with the bulk of the goods are all east of here." Kate shaded her eyes with her parasol and looked east, then west, trying to make out the flags. "At the end I see a red one, with a white cross ... that would be Denmark. And the tricolour of France. Spain is yellow with red. The United States of America has all the stars and stripes, and Sweden is the blue with a yellow cross ... No wonder it seems European here! And are there some factories under construction?"

"Over by the market, perhaps," Sir Tom replied, obviously remembering her need to take images of any new buildings. "I'll show you later, but I think it will be in the other ports you'll find more subject matter."

"What's that about?" Mrs. Farewell asked.

"I'm planning on creating a portfolio of the European construction in each Chinese port we visit," Kate said, trying to sound casual.

"Why?"

"To show people at home what other nations are doing out here. I believe they'll find it interesting."

"Not as interesting as the Oriental sights in general. You could capture images of everything. How many plates do you have? It would all —"

"We have to go to the Chowchow Factory," Kate interrupted, changing the subject and feeling excited. "The infirmary is supposed to be at the north end of Hog Lane, wherever that is."

"Hog Lane is this opening right here," Sir Tom said, pointing ahead. "And this is the Chowchow Factory, but we're not going up the lane, it's too rough. We'll go around the block, over to Old China Street. This is the American Garden we're passing. That was the British Garden behind us."

"Where's Chowchow?" Mrs. Farewell asked. "It's not a country I've ever heard of."

"No, it's not," Sir Tom said, and chuckled. "I think it has Chinese owners. 'Chowchow' is a jargon term. It would roughly translate as miscellaneous. It's one of the poorer establishments. Cheaper products, cheap labour for hire. There's the Creek Factory, the Imperial Factory ... and they all have several names. Like the Old English Factory is also Lung-shun Hong, which means Gloriously Prosperous Factory."

They walked along the front of six buildings, beside a park enclosure, then turned and went through a covered gate onto a busy, narrow road paved with flagstones. The atmosphere changed immediately to close and crowded. The jutting-out upper stories had windows with lattice shutters, and overhead ropes filled with drying laundry stretched across. At several spots were covered walkways spanning the road like little bridges. There were no windows on the ground floor, just open doorways with a single step. Beside each a placard was posted with Chinese calligraphy and a fancy lantern (gold with red glass was very popular). Every section had elaborately painted panels depicting dragons, tigers, landscapes, and other such art.

Kate started to see native men up close, and realized they were staring briefly at her as they passed. Porters carried huge loads, going in or out of the many doorways, but mostly hurrying along at a trot to unknown destinations, probably the waterfront. Their bundles, easily twice the size of the porters, were covered with plain cloth and bound by ropes. The men balanced the ponderous loads on their backs and strained against leather straps running across their breasts or foreheads. Many used long poles and carried two smaller loads dangling from the ends, bouncing as they jogged. Despite the obvious effort being exerted, some men paused to smile at each other and say a few words before hurrying off again. They all seemed quite content in their labour. There were idlers, however, scruffy filthy men who tried to follow Kate and touch her, but her grandfather kept scaring them off. They reached the end of the road. A broad street ran east and west with a high reddish brown wall blocking the way into the city.

"This is Thirteen Factories Street," Sir Tom said over the din of chatter, firecrackers, and gongs. "Stay to the side. If you see a sedan chair, don't get in the way."

"What do you mean?" Mrs. Farewell asked.

"The mandarins, the wealthy elite, ride in sedan chairs," Sir Tom explained. "They look like little fancy houses being carried by porters. Here's one now. Oh, two, actually."

Coming along the middle of the street, each carried with staves by four men in red silk, were box-like structures covered in gold. They did indeed look like little houses with curved pagoda roofs and pillars at the corners, decorated with fantastic beasts

and intricately carved lattice windows and doors. Kate tried to
see in, curious as to what a mandarin might look like, but she
was foiled by the lining behind the lattices. On the north side
of the street, running along the wall, was a strip of pavement
the Europeans and wealthy Chinese seemed to dominate. Kate
could see some native men in long silk robes of many bright colours
and round velvet hats of varying styles.

"Let's carry on," she said.

Kate skipped through the crowds and onto the pavement. She
quickened her pace, but then caught herself.

"Please walk faster, Grandfather, we're arriving without an
appointment. You have to make the inquiries for me."

"You're not in England." Sir Tom waved her on. "Go ahead.
You're safe on this street, and we're both tall enough to see each
other. We'll keep in sight and soon catch you up. Stop at the top
of Hog Lane."

"Oh ... all right!" Kate smiled. "I rather like leading the way."

Suddenly she was beside three stunning young Chinese ladies
wrapped in bright red and white satin robes extensively embroidered with colourful birds and flowers that covered them from
throat to ankle, their wooden sandals clicking as they walked.
Voluminous sleeves draped past their hands, through which they
held paper parasols with similarly painted adornments. Their
sleek black hair was piled upon their heads and held with bejewelled combs, except for the braid at the back. They all stopped and
looked at one another for a moment, Kate peering at the embroidery, the ladies seemingly taken by her gold outfit, or perhaps her
fancy plaits and wavy hair cascading about her shoulders and
down her back.

"Hello?" she ventured. *This is what I expected!*

The trio bowed. Kate started to curtsy, but then bowed in
turn, taking a closer look at their footwear and noting the thick
white silk hose they were wearing. *These ladies have small feet,
but I thought they'd be tiny, from binding. I suppose they aren't*

of that class ... they appear extremely wealthy. I wonder what their undergarments are like? The robes are exquisite, but those sandals don't look very comfortable. She realized the ladies were now eyeing her oddly, with little frowns. *Oh dear, I'm being rude, staring at their feet.* Kate smiled, pointed a toe, and pulled her skirt and petticoats up just enough to reveal her finely crafted boot, the embroidered cuff of her expensive stocking, and part of her white silk hose, similar to theirs. They peered for a moment, then smiled and nodded, apparently appreciative of Kate's clothing and her attempt to show a small similarity in their dress, then they promenaded away.

When Kate found what she believed was the north opening of Hog Lane, she stood back out of the way and tried to spot some kind of medical clinic. At the corner was a shop with an open front. Women sat on a carpet, bent over garments, making repairs. They wore large round spectacles that created owl-like visages. Some of them had tiny pointed feet. *So it's not just wealthy women who bind their feet? But not all wealthy women. It's like any fashion, I suppose, but mothers decide for their daughters?* Sir Tom and Mrs. Farewell approached on the other side of the street. He waved above the crowd and pointed to a nearby doorway. Kate hurried over to them, and they entered the back of the Chowchow Factory.

Inside was like a crowded covered alley with skylights, the shops facing inward, most with open doors, some with open fronts. To their right was a plain establishment, litters leaning in a row outside the door. Two young Chinese women stood outside. They were wearing silk shirts and trousers, worn dull from use, and had their long straight black hair braided at the back, except for a small portion at the front cut straight across at their eyebrows. Approaching them, Kate found that while not richly adorned like the passing trio they were quite delicate and lovely, with small features, large dark eyes, and clear skin.

"Hello?" she asked, not knowing if they would understand her.

"Hello," the women responded softly with a thick accent.

"Is this Mr. Tattersall's infirmary?"

"Yes, Doctor Henry is here."

Kate smiled and folded her parasol. "I'm an acquaintance of his from England, Lady Katelyn Beaufort. These are my chaperones." She turned and held a hand towards Sir Tom and Mrs. Farewell. "Do you understand what I'm saying? Would you take me to Dr. Tattersall, please?"

The women glanced at each other, then studied Kate for a moment.

"This way," one of them said, and darted inside.

Kate followed, passing through a thick wall, finding it darker and cooler within. She looked back to see Mrs. Farewell close behind, and her grandfather having to stoop to get through the door.

"This way," the woman called from the end of the white-washed hall.

Kate hurried to keep up, stepping quickly along the polished grey flagstones. She passed open doors that revealed wards. There was at least one shaded window in each room, allowing enough light to see the cots. European and Chinese staff, male and female, tended to the sick. A feeling of apprehension crept into her breast.

What do these people have? She started to take shallow breaths. *Oh dear, I'm afraid I might catch the contagion.*

The air seemed fresh enough, but she started to perceive sour tints, like unwashed bodies mixed with vinegar. Reaching the end of the hall, there were several small chambers. One appeared to be an examination room, brightly lit by ambient light from many thin white fabric windows, and a similar space appeared to be some kind of laboratory. Beside it was a dark room the woman disappeared into. A moment later the shade opened. Kate stood in the doorway, afraid to enter.

Something's not right ...

"Doctor Henry," the woman said gently. "Doctor Henry, you awake?"

"Yes, what is it, Liu?" The voice sounded weak.

Kate edged towards the cot. *Oh no, he's ill.* She noticed a sharp pang in her breast, a lump in her stomach.

"An English noblewoman is come see you."

"Pardon?"

"It's me, Dr. Tattersall." Kate strode to his bedside. "Lady Katelyn Beaufort ... Kate."

"Ah, Kate ... yes, Beaufort's little sister." He sat up a bit. "I'm afraid I've caught one of the illnesses I've been attempting to cure." He lay covered with blankets and trembling, sweat beaded on his forehead, his eyes yellow.

"He has a fever attacking his liver." A bald man of about forty entered the room, talking with a slight German accent. "I am Dr. Dressens. I share this sick house with Henry."

"What's to be done?" Kate asked. *Is he going to die?*

"He's the miracle worker," Dr. Dressens declared, leaning over Henry and feeling his forehead. "I must see to my other patients. Excuse me."

"May I be alone with him for a moment?" Kate asked.

Sir Tom took Mrs. Farewell by the elbow and guided her into the hall. Liu followed.

Kate hesitated, then perched on the edge of the cot. "How long have you been unwell?"

"Ten days, I believe." He gave her a small smile. "The days and nights have somewhat blurred together. I was like this about a year ago, but not as severe. I've only been back here about six weeks." He took a deep breath and sighed. "Is your brother with you?"

"No, I'm visiting with my grandfather," Kate said, her throat getting tight, her voice failing. *He looks so weak, so very weak ...* She felt a tear run down her cheek and turned away, not wanting him to see her upset. Opening her handbag she pulled out a perfumed handkerchief and the envelope for Henry. "I have a very important missive for you. I believe it may be from Lord Palmerston? Do you ... are you employed by Foreign Affairs?"

"Let me see the note." He held up a trembling hand.

"I'll have to open it for you."

Kate took out her silver fruit knife and cut the waxed cloth. Using her hands, concentrating on a task, allowed her to regain composure. Inside she found another envelope of similarly treated paper. She tore it open and within was a letter, sealed with black. *How odd, mourning wax?* Breaking the seal, she unfolded the leaf and handed it to Henry. Kate watched him read it over several times, then he collapsed back on his pillow. She peeked at the writing, but it just looked like a jumble of random words.

It must be a code. What was the word Palmerston used when we met? Ah, yes! "Is this about taskings for Foreign Affairs?" Kate asked, trying to quell the excitement in her voice.

"Yes, the Secret Service," Henry whispered.

"The Secret Service? Foreign Affairs operatives who carry out clandestine taskings? Henry, aren't you in Canton for your medical work? Are you an operative?"

"How much do you know?"

"I'm not sure I should say," Kate replied, thinking of how her brother had insisted everything be kept secret. *Damn you Jack! You should be here!* "I ... I know my brother works for ... works for Pam. And I met with him before leaving London."

"Good enough. You brought a package with you?"

"Yes, one of Jack's long-range rifles," Kate said, nodding.

"I'll need you to deliver it for me."

"It's not for you?"

"No. Take it to Wu at the New English Factory. He's a manager there, and speaks proper English. Not the pidgin jargon so many people use here."

"Can you describe him?" *Oh my, I have to teach a stranger how to shoot? A man to whom I haven't been properly introduced?*

"No, we've never met, but the rifle is for him. To execute a man who is an embarrassment to the Crown."

"Execute an embarrassment? Odds zounds! That sounds a bit extreme."

"He's smuggling huge quantities of opium through Canton into mainland China, and taking slaves out."

Kate bristled all over. "Slavery is a great evil, and must be stopped at all costs! An Englishman, doing this?"

"Yes, Mr. Aloysius James Napier. He came out here as a merchant, but he's a slaver and smuggler now."

"Wish Napier? Of the Sussex Square Napiers?"

"Yes. Ah, you know him? Pam probably thought of that." Henry nodded slowly, shifting on his pillow.

"What of it? Why would Palmerston think of this? Yes, I know him. He comes from very good people. We use the same mews when we're in London." Kate thought of a gregarious man, about the same age as her brother. "He helped with my saddle many times, when I was waiting for a groom, and our families rode the parks together on Saturdays a few times every season. I haven't seen him for several years."

"He came here with all the funds he needed to equip a small army. He's a warlord now."

"Perhaps this is a mistake," Kate suggested.

"There's no mistake." Henry closed his eyes. "Please take the rifle to Wu."

"I will." Kate stood. "And I'm going to see about taking you back to England."

He opened his eyes, but seemed unable to focus. "Pardon?"

"Henry," she said, bending over him, placing one hand on his breast and wiping his face with her handkerchief. "You're sick, and need help. Let me help you."

"Kate, my work ..."

"Your work can be continued in England, once you're well again. I'm going to make arrangements for you. You are strong enough to travel? Please say yes."

"Yes," he sighed and closed his eyes, then whispered, "My parents would like me to stay at home."

Kate lingered over him for a moment, taking in his drawn but still handsome features. She folded her handkerchief so the embroidered initials, KEB, were on top, placed it on his bedside table, hoping he would think of her when he saw it, then slipped silently from the room. The hall was empty. Hurrying to the entrance, Kate found Sir Tom and Mrs. Farewell waiting outside. She quickly told them the situation in regards to Henry, and her intentions.

"Are you certain? You barely know the lad," Sir Tom observed. "This spoils your grand tour."

"I know," Kate replied. "I'll travel again someday. I cannot leave Dr. Tattersall here and go sightseeing. It would be selfish."

"Spoken like a grown woman," Mrs. Farewell said, raising an eyebrow. "In fact, like a wife, thinking about her man, putting him first. Is there something between you two?"

"No ... but I do care for him, Nanny. I told Grandfather on the way here, but nobody else knows, except perhaps Jack. Anyway, he's a righteous young man who wants only to help the sick, and now he's been struck down. I'll gladly give up my tour to help him."

"Goodness, that's the same kind of sacrifice you'll have to make for children. You're really growing up."

"Thank you. I didn't think of it that way."

"Let me see if I can find him passage on a Royal Navy vessel through to Bombay," Sir Tom suggested. "They sail day and night out in the open sea, and he would have the care of the ship's surgeon on the way. There's a fine hospital in Bombay, Kate. If he's well enough to carry on, we'll try to take him from there."

"That's sage advice, child," Mrs. Farewell said firmly. "It's better you don't get any further attached to him. Not yet."

"Oh ... yes." Kate thought a moment. *They think he'll die at sea. Then into the cold dark depths, how awful ... No, he'll live.* "Can you arrange this today?"

"Perhaps. Let's get back to the boat," Sir Tom said. "I'll change into my uniform and see about finding a berth for the lad."

"Thank you, Grandfather."

CHAPTER 10

A FACTORY AND A WAREHOUSE

Sir Tom donned his dress uniform and marched off looking for representatives of the Admiralty. Kate changed too, into her pink outfit, wanting to preserve the gold suit for special occasions. She was determined to make her delivery as soon as possible. When she climbed on deck with the rifle, Colonel Bob stood by the rail, watching some crewmen load supplies.

Kate approached him. "Would you please accompany me to the New English Factory? I have to deliver this case to a man who works there."

"In a moment, girl," he said, nodding. "I'll carry it for you." He took the case and strode about the deck ordering the men what to do, then came back to her.

Kate led him down the gangplank, taking his arm, and they strolled to the row of factories. Colonel Bob guided her past the Chowchow Factory to the building next door, on the other side of Hog Lane.

"This is the New English Factory?"

"Aye," Colonel Bob said. "It's the largest. Twice as big as most of them. I think the East India Company owns it."

"We were in the one beside it earlier, but at the other end."

"Oh? Some go all the way through down the middle, with courtyards, some don't. It can take a long time to walk through a factory."

"Somewhere in there is a man named Wu." *Oh dear, this may take awhile.*

"Is that all you know about him?"

"He's a manager, and he speaks decent English."

They approached the front doors, where men, mostly natives carrying small parcels or envelopes, were going in and out. A very tall Chinese man in a red tunic and brown vest, holding a musket and wearing a long dagger, barred their way.

"No fenqui woman," he said.

"We visit short time," Colonel Bob snapped. "Contentee?"

"No. Takee fenqui woman, go. "

"What's wrong?" Kate asked.

"He's a constable," Colonel Bob explained. "He must have orders not to let European women in."

"What does 'fenqui' mean?"

"Foreign devil."

"My goodness! Foreign devil?"

A passing young gentleman, neatly dressed with spectacles, a dark complexion, and ink-spattered hands, obviously having heard Kate's exclamation, laughed and stopped.

"Hello there, chap," Colonel Bob said. "Work inside here?"

"Si," the man responded, then added with a thick accent, "I am a clerk."

"Oh." *How odd to find a Spaniard working in the New English Factory.* Kate asked in her most polite Spanish if he knew a manager named Wu.

The man responded by telling Kate she was the most beautiful woman in Canton.

"Gracias," Kate said quietly, embarrassed. She noticed Colonel Bob looking at her with a raised eyebrow and translated what the clerk had said.

"Well, I think he's right." Colonel Bob shrugged and winked. "At least, the most beautiful girl. But if he gives you any cheek you let me know. I'll sort him —"

"No, no, por favor!" The man held up his hands, grinning sheepishly. "No need for that. Wu is the manager of the silk storeroom in this factory. It's near this end of the building."

"The constable won't let us pass," Kate said.

"I'll fix it." The clerk declared something in Chinese, handed over some coins, then held the door open wide. "Adelante, come in! You are now my sister and grandfather visiting from Cadiz. The soldado will show you to the silk store."

Inside looked rather like Old China Street, except grander, cleaner, and even busier, the work going on along a series of second-floor balconies as well.

"Gracias, señor." Kate curtsied.

"Ah, dios mio," the man sighed. "My pleasure, señorita." He bowed, then turned away and disappeared into the crowd.

"Wasn't that nice of him," Kate said. "I wonder why he helped us so readily?"

"Ha! You turned his head, girl," Colonel Bob replied. "I think you'll find for at least the next ten years young men will be doing you favours all the time. Come on, let's make good use of our fierce guide."

The constable led them at a quick pace, the masses parting for him. For about eighty feet the interior had some resemblance to a British banking house, but then there was a courtyard and beyond it the usual painted wood and lanterns, shops only on the ground floor. A noticeable difference was the placards outside the doors: both Chinese and English, with bold letters announcing tea, ivory, preserves, flowerpot stands, and on and on. Just past the airy open square, the constable pointed out a door with a placard reading "Silk", and stomped off.

They made their way into a long room full of the valuable fabric, roll after roll in every colour, counters covered with piles of swatches. A tiny old man with a flowing white beard knotted at the bottom, wearing a faded blue-grey robe and jacket, came towards them with small, quick steps. His little round black cap had embroidered symbols on it. He carried a long pointer, which he waved in their direction.

"Are you buyers?" he asked sharply.

"No," Kate began, and before she could say another word he'd already turned away. "Wait! I'm looking for a man named Wu. Do you know him?"

The man turned back. "I am Wu."

"Oh, uh, Mr. Wu." *Good Lord, he looks ninety years old.* Kate took the rifle from Colonel Bob, did a little curtsy, then drew close and lowered her voice almost to a whisper. "I've come from England, and I was instructed to give you this case." She stood head and shoulders taller than the Chinese man, so she bent over and talked, peering into his cloudy brown eyes. He stared back for a moment, completely still.

"You do not call me Mr. Wu," he burst out sharply. "Just Wu. I call you Lotus Blossom, you are pink like flowers. Do not tell me your name."

"I don't always wear pink. Why can't you know my name?"

"So no matter what happen to me, I do not say who you are."

"Are you in danger? What might —"

"Come away from your man."

"Just give me a moment, Colonel Murray," Kate said, then followed Wu to the end of the counter.

"What you have in box?" Wu asked.

"A rifle."

Wu glanced at the case and screwed up his face like there was a bad smell.

"And it's a very unique weapon, for shooting great distances," Kate tried to explain. "I cannot take it out here, with all these people around."

"Rifle don't fit in there," Wu insisted, tapping the case with his pointer.

"Oh, yes, now I understand why you look doubtful. It breaks down into three pieces, but assembles very quickly. I'll show you how to use it?" *He'll never be able to handle it, he's so old and small.*

"Why you show me this?"

"Ah ... I believe you're going to execute a man? This will allow you to do it from far away. So no one knows you did it?"

"You talk about Englishman? Napier?"

"Yes." *I still cannot believe it's Wish Napier.* "Do you know him? What has he been doing in China?"

"He do evil work! Corrupt!" Wu spat.

"You're certain of this?"

"I show you. Leave your man here."

"Will we be long?" *I don't like this, but I am curious.*

"We be quick."

Kate handed the case back to Colonel Bob, looked at him wide-eyed and shrugged, then said, "I'll just go with this man for a moment. Then perhaps he'll take this delivery and we can be on our way."

"You go with him? Not a chance," Colonel Bob said flatly.

"I'll be fine. There are soldiers everywhere outside."

"Aye, that's true. All right then."

Wu turned, yelled at some workers while waving his pointer, and started for an exit at the back of the storeroom. Kate followed, puzzled as to where he would lead her. Outside, they navigated a tight, dirty alley, then headed east, crossed a little bridge over a creek, and entered a maze of warehouses. Clearly this wasn't an area frequented by European women, and Kate felt keenly aware of the looks she received.

Oh damn, we've already left the troops far behind. Wu led her to a tiny door, which he pulled open and passed inside. *Maybe I should just go back?* She listened for a moment: it sounded silent within. *Hmm, I'll just have a quick look.* Having to stoop to enter, she fought past a musty curtain and found herself in a long, low, dark room, light filtering in from only a few small windows. Hundreds of intricately carved dark wooden chests, each about the size of a tea caddy or hat box, filled the space.

"Look, look," Wu whispered, opening a lid. "You come see."

Kate peered in and saw it was full of rolled leaves forming balls, some partially open revealing thumb-sized wads of black putty. "What is this?"

"Opium."

She turned and opened another, then another; they were all full of opium. Even with her gloves on she didn't like touching the chests.

"This is all Napier's?" she exclaimed.

"Why, yes, 'tis indeed," an Irish lilt spoke from a dark corner. "However, I'd be happy to sell you some, if that's what you have in mind, so I would."

A man of average height and solid build, dressed in beige light cotton clothing with scuffed knee-high brown boots, a heavy cavalry sabre on his hip, approached with a lopsided smile.

"I'm not interested, thank you." *The outrage! I must not let my feelings show.* She noticed Wu slip back behind the curtain. *Where are you going? Wu! Come back!*

"Archie Cavanagh, at your service." The Irishman gave a bow. He had steely eyes, a low brow, light rusty hair, and appeared to be in his mid-thirties.

Kate curtsied without thinking, caught herself halfway, and straightened. "Ah, Mr. Cavanagh, you are ... are you in Mr. Napier's employ?"

"My, how formal. We're not in high society here. Call me Archie. And you are?" He drew nearer.

Kate, her eyes grown accustomed to the light, could see a deep, jagged scar arching over his left cheek from ear to chin. *He looks dangerous.* "I'm ... I'm just visiting." *Hmm, not bad. I have to talk my way out of here.* "Do you take care of shipping these chests?"

"I tend to many tasks. That's a lovely outfit. Did you get it in London?"

"It's not so nice. How long have you been in China?"

"A while. How long have you been in Canton?"

"I'm just passing through." *We're both avoiding each other's questions.* The verbal jousting was getting nowhere, and Kate felt anxious. Cavanagh, meanwhile, looked absolutely at ease, his crooked smile giving him a slightly amused expression.

"Thank you for your time, Mr. Cavanagh, but I must be on —"

"Palmerston isn't sending ladies now, is he?"

Palmerston? That caught Kate by surprise. She'd started to turn away, but stopped. *What does he know? How do I counter such a question?* "Why, whatever do you mean?" Kate tried to ask without sounding too interested.

"For every straight answer you give me, I'll return the favour. A fair arrangement, wouldn't you agree?" He edged closer and smiled.

Is he toying with me? "I suppose." *I don't know if this is wise, but I do want answers.*

"Your name?"

"I'm … Mrs. Tattersall." *There, if he believes I'm married he won't get randy, I hope. I'll tell him lies and get clear of this predicament.* "All this opium, is it to be smuggled into China?"

"Oh yes, lots of buyers here. Did you come recently from London?"

"Yes. I've also heard Mr. Napier deals in slaves, is that true?"

"Yes, fairly common in China. Did Palmerston ask you to come looking for Napier's opium?"

"You're an opium smuggler and a slave trader?" Kate could barely keep her loathing hidden. She was hot; her muscles tightened, and her insides trembled. Confusion struck her as well. *There he goes asking about Palmerston again.*

"You just broke our agreement." Cavanagh appeared hurt, frowned a bit and raised an eyebrow, then shrugged it off. "But I will do you the honour of a response. I'm neither. I'm a professional soldier. Napier employs me to train and discipline his troops."

"A mercenary, and you're paid with gold from opium and slaves?"

"Not much different from when I was in the Royal Engineers. One paymaster guilty of atrocities is as good as another."

"You were in the British Army?" *You're a liar and a scoundrel, no doubt!*

"Indeed, and a lovely time I had." Cavanagh's crooked smile spread into a wide grin, his scar wrinkling.

"I must be going." Kate felt this had gone on long enough, and she needed to think things over. "It was a delight meeting you, Mr. Cavanagh." *Ha! I can lie too.* She quickly stepped back to the curtain and passed out the door.

As she pushed it closed, she heard faintly, "Aye, sweet lady, a delight."

Back out in the sunlight, Kate saw Wu standing at the corner twiddling the end of his beard. He waved his pointer and started heading back to the factories. Kate ran to catch up with him.

"How can all that opium just be sitting there?" she demanded. "Anyone could take it."

"No one touch. Napier too dangerous."

"Your Emperor has thousands of troops. He could put an end to this."

"Our divine Emperor try to stop you devils from bringing opium here. Your soldiers come and forced it on us."

Oh dear. This is horrible. Now I understand why Foreign Affairs wants Napier stopped. The Chinese just see us all as foreign devils, bringing opium here, and slavery. Something must be done! "Is there someone I can teach to use the rifle? Someone you know who's young and strong?"

"How long will it take?"

"Perhaps a day, depending on the pupil. We'd have to find a secluded valley, and —"

"And how this young strong man know what Napier look like?"

"Ah, yes, it would have to be someone who can recognize —"

"No! You English have to kill Napier."

"Why?"

"He your devil. You know him?"

"Yes."

"You know how to work special gun?"

"Yes." *Oh no ...*

"Then you know how to kill him!"

How did it come to this? Jack should be here ... but he can't shoot. Was Henry supposed to execute Wish Napier? No, he said the rifle had to be delivered to Wu. Palmerston knew I was coming here with the rifle! What did Henry say?

"You find out where Napier is, then you kill him," Wu insisted.

"You don't even know where he is?" *I don't think I can do this.*

"He move around. Sometime here, sometime there."

They entered the silk storeroom. Colonel Bob approached. Wu stopped and peered up at her.

"You help us, Lotus Blossom? Take away opium warlord?"

Oh dear. Could I do such a deed? It would be justice. I need to go over all this. I don't even know if he's here. "Is there a way to locate Mr. Napier? Without him knowing I'm searching for him?" Kate watched the old man as he studied his slippers for a moment, tapping his pointer. "Surely there is some way to —"

"Be quiet and listen," he said, cutting her off. "I take you to dream room tomorrow at sunset. Meet me here. Come quiet to door in alley."

"Very good, whither shall —"

"Now go away!"

Colonel Bob moved up beside Kate. "Just a moment there, what's all —"

"Go now!" Wu yelled over his shoulder, then scurried off and started to harangue some workers in his native tongue.

"I've still got this case," Colonel Bob said with raised eyebrows.

"Yes, I'm keeping it, for now. Thank you for waiting. Let's go back to the boat."

❖

Sunset brought Sir Tom's return. In the gloaming his very dark blue uniform appeared black, but the eight-pointed silver star of his knighthood, Army Gold Cross with bars, and other medals still glittered. Kate wanted to ask what each was for, but other subjects weighed heavily on her mind.

"I've found a frigate leaving for India in two days," he announced. "The captain approved, and the surgeon is happy to take Dr. Tattersall into his care. So there you go."

"Thank you, Grandfather, this is good news. I'll visit him tomorrow morning and find out what needs to be packed." She drew him towards the bow to talk in privacy. "There have been other complications."

Kate ran over everything: what Henry had said, and what had happened upon visiting Wu. Spelling it all out, listening to her own reasoning, she decided Napier should be dealt with.

"So you're embroiled in some kind of Secret Service covert operation for Palmerston," Sir Tom said, shaking his head.

"Apparently. Have you heard of the Secret Service before?"

"Yes, but I'm not familiar with their work. I don't particularly care for cloak and dagger. The spies we used during the wars with France formed the organization. My understanding is they fall under Army High Command, but perhaps Foreign Affairs directs them."

"It's hard to fathom how I got mixed up in this." *Did Jack and Palmerston plan this?*

"And you're going to let this man Wu take you to a dream room?" Sir Tom asked with a skeptical look on his face.

"Yes. What is a dream room?"

"An opium den."

"Oh no ... I didn't know that. I still have to go. I wonder if it belongs to Mr. Napier?"

"Might well be. He could have several in the city. But he probably moves most of his opium inland. That's where he'd get his slaves."

"What a shameful disgrace. An English gentleman involved in such scandalous industries," Kate said, feeling angry. "He deserves to be punished. I believe it in my heart, and feel perhaps I'm the person to do it."

"You were a wild, mischievous child," Sir Tom said, shaking his head. "I remember visiting when you were about six. All you wanted to talk about was great adventures. Is this what you meant?"

"No. I don't know what I meant. Is this a great adventure? I never really thought it through."

"Let me do the task," Sir Tom suggested.

"You don't know Mr. Napier. Or how to use the rifle. It's not like anything you've handled before. Adjusting the telescope is tricky."

"It has a telescope?"

"Yes, because it can shoot accurately so far."

"What do you intend? Climb around the roofs of the city? Or shoot him from a window?"

"I guess so. Something like that."

"You really believe you'd be able? I don't question your skill to make the shot, I mean to shoot dead a childhood acquaintance."

"I don't know."

"And dressed in that sweet pink outfit?"

"Oh dear, these clothes have come up again and again today. I have a beige riding habit. You saw it, when we were in Suez. It would be less noticeable."

"But still silk, so it shines in the sun. Just teach me how to use the rifle, Kate."

"I have been intending on showing it to you, and almost delivered it today without doing so. Actually, now that you know everything, maybe we don't need the rifle at all! Why don't we apprehend Mr. Napier together?" *Yes, that's it!* "You can speak to him as a knight, representing the Crown, explain the situation, and bring him to justice. I remember him as a perfectly reasonable gentleman."

"Do you?" Sir Tom said quietly, looking out at the city. "Hmm, well, let's keep thinking it over. Tomorrow, after we visit your young man, we'll talk some more."

"All right."

"Good. Let's have some dinner."

AN OPIUM DEN

The next morning after breakfast, Kate, Mrs. Farewell, and Sir Tom made the trip to the infirmary. Henry hovered in and out of delirium, mumbling about needed supplies, laundry schedules, and cremation of the dead. He only had two chests to fill with clothes and books. Dr. Dressens, who was very busy, took time to show them the medicine required, a dose Henry had prescribed for himself. Kate blinked back tears while packing, stopping every few minutes to check Henry, dabbing his forehead with a wet cloth.

After, Sir Tom led them to where a market was set up near the Danish Factory. Stalls, all green-painted wood with little doorways, tended to by Chinese merchants in embroidered robes, stood in lines stretching for hundreds of feet. Finely dressed Europeans strolled up and down the lines, stopping and bartering prices. The merchants would lure customers in and close the door, then a muffled palaver of the pidgin lingo would continue. Kate discerned many accents, but the exclamations of the French ladies, obviously delighted by the selection, were the loudest, except occasionally when a German or Russian gentleman called out.

"You said something about wanting to explore some markets?" Sir Tom asked.

"Yes, I did, and this is beyond my imagination. I could spend days here," Kate said, after peeking in several doorways and taking in the merchandise, a myriad of exotic wooden and stone carvings, vases, chests, paintings, kites, mirrors, clothing, parasols, swords, spices, perfumes, incense ... there was no end to it, each stall specializing in a certain product. "But somehow I'm not so enthusiastic anymore. I've got too much on my mind. Although, I don't know if I can resist the striped wooden tiger in that last shop."

"Well, at least step in here for a minute." He indicated a nearby doorway. Upon entering it became immediately evident, due to the countless samples of cloth and patterns, that a tailoring business was housed within. A pair of Chinese men bowed and then waited with raised eyebrows and small smiles, nodding their heads expectantly.

"Chin-chin," they said.

"Chin-chin," Sir Tom responded, bowing, and motioned to his beige light cotton breeches and jacket. He pointed at Kate. "Outfit. For young miss, chop-chop."

"What's this about, Grandfather?"

"You need some field clothes." He winked.

"Oh, I see, yes." Kate considered her pink outfit and liked the idea. *If I am going to accompany Grandfather when he confronts Napier, being dressed like a man would be wise. I might have to do some climbing or running, and I certainly don't want to have to do that in a skirt again.* "An excellent idea. Thank you."

"You can't wear such clothes!" Mrs. Farewell gasped. "I won't allow it."

"They would only be for special circumstances," Kate said softly, feeling a bit miffed for being talked to in such a fashion with the men watching.

"It's just like when you were a child. The escapades you got into. I won't have —"

"Nanny, please," Kate cut her off. "You're right, of course. I promise there will be no foolishness, but I am having this suit made."

"Fine." The older woman set her jaw and glanced around with narrowed eyes. "I'll wait outside. I've got some of my own shopping to do."

"How long will it take?" Kate asked while the men noted her shape with knotted strings.

"It will probably be finished by sometime tomorrow. The suits are already made. They'll just alter one to fit you. The seamstresses will work through the night."

"Excellent." She smiled. "These people are certainly industrious. Then I would like to go into the market. For a wide-brimmed canvas hat, to match the outfit. And the stall we just passed with the stone carvings, let's have a look there. I believe it's mostly jade, and I saw a great deal of horses."

"Very good." Sir Tom grinned. "I'm glad you're getting a small chance to enjoy this."

❖

In the afternoon Kate, though apprehensive, decided to test Jack's camera. She walked along the waterfront casually looking for a subject while two of the *Otter*'s old crewmen trailed about twenty paces behind, content to act as escorts. Jack's device was small, and was carried like a handbag, so no one seemed to notice. She couldn't find any construction being carried out by a European country, so she selected a new boathouse for a preliminary attempt. The wooden structure was long and narrow, with red pillars holding up a gently sloping clay tile roof, echoing the architecture of the pagodas. She furtively glanced into the view aperture, opened the lens cover, counted to five, then snapped the cover closed and strolled away, suspecting it would be a decent image except for the blurs caused by people moving about. Kate, happy at how well it had gone, felt doing the process on buildings under construction should be easy. It might prove tedious, walking back and forth to look after the plates, but ensuring they went into the proper envelopes quickly was essential. It was quite a pleasant little task, and a welcome distraction from the whole Napier business and having to meet Wu later.

"Grandfather," she called out when climbing on deck. "How

many Chinese ports shall we visit? All five? I'll want to get to Bombay as quickly as possible."

"Fine. Perhaps we won't go as far as Shanghai."

"We have to reach Ningpo. There's the Bibles to deliver."

"Ah, yes. Well, Shanghai is only about fifteen leagues farther north, so I guess we'll go there too."

"As long as we're quick," Kate agreed. "I did tell Jack I would get the images."

"We'll do our best." Sir Tom leaned on the rail and spoke softly, "Tell me, are you still planning on meeting this Wu character at sundown? Haven't changed your mind?"

"No, I'll meet with him. I said I would. It will allow me to find out where Mr. Napier is currently. Then perhaps we'll have a talk with him?"

"Make him see the error of his ways, eh? You better get something to eat," Sir Tom said, staring off to the west. "There isn't much time."

"Yes, right." Kate hurried to the galley.

When she emerged, Sir Tom and Colonel Bob stood on the deck talking in low voices. She was glad Mrs. Farewell seemed nowhere in sight, so wouldn't ask any questions.

"I'll be back presently," she said while passing the men.

Colonel Bob started to say something, but Sir Tom stopped him.

"Be careful, Kate."

"I will, Grandfather."

She stepped lightly down the gangplank and followed the path beside the church, happy to see a detachment of British soldiers patrolling the waterfront. Checking the progress of the sun's decline, she half ran to the silk storeroom at the New English Factory. *I mustn't be late, Wu is cantankerous enough already.*

Kate scampered up the alley and tried the door, found it locked, but even before she'd taken her hand from the knob it was opened from within. Wu peered out, and then beckoned to her. He led her with short, quick steps through the long room to a side hall with a series of offices. Still not saying a word he directed her to a large closet. A lantern lit the inside, and on a chair sat a set of blue satin clothes and cream-coloured slippers.

"You get changed," Wu said quietly and closed her in.

Kate hesitated just a moment before disrobing, keeping on her chemise and hose, then donned the outfit: shirt, trousers, slippers, all fitting comfortably. They weren't new, but were fresh and clean. She raced through the process, trembling, feeling her stomach tighten. *Does everyone who goes to an opium den have to wear these clothes?* She opened the door and found Wu standing at the threshold holding a brush and a basin of water.

"Your hair must be flat, Lotus Blossom," he snapped.

"Ah, right." Kate could see where this was going. *He wants me to look Chinese. It's just lucky my hair is black.* She untied her tresses, hands shaking and muscles tight, and quickly wet and brushed them out, hoping the waves cascading to her waist would hang fairly straight. When she set the brush down, Wu grabbed her hair and expertly braided it, tying the bottom with a red ribbon. He handed her a little blue cap, similar to the one he wore and Kate had seen throughout Canton since she'd arrived. The small man glanced her up and down, then started along the hall and out another door, back into the alley. He led her to the north end of the factories and they entered the notorious Hog Lane, passing close to the infirmary, night falling around them, gongs ringing out all over the city. Men of every race, wearing the varied garb of sailors, were stumbling about, laughing loudly, singing, gambling, and fighting. The lane was like a long, dirty outdoor tavern, reeking of alcohol and urine. Wu and Kate had to dash by the knots of men, being careful not to pause near any of the rambunctious gangs. Several times she nimbly passed her guide and had to cower in a doorway, watching for him to work through the crowds. Soon they were at the mouth of a dark passage. With every step Kate grew more apprehensive. *I can always turn back. In this outfit I could run like the wind.*

"When you get in dream room, you do as told and listen," Wu advised quietly. "Barbarians in brown work for Napier. Men of his come every night. They may say if in city, or away, or somewhere. They speak many odd languages. You understand?"

"Wait, Mr. Wu, I'm frightened ... I'm afraid this isn't going to work!" Kate felt herself trembling, her muscles coiling, like she could jump over buildings or sprint back to the *Otter* in a flash. Her heart throbbed, pounding in her breast and temples. "I don't look Chinese enough."

"Do not call me 'Mister.'" Wu shook his head, his beard swaying. "You will be dream. Men in there ride dragon. Some ride high, some low. You will be dream to them all. Do not let men touch you."

Into the dark passage, they stole up to a black door. Wu did some kind of twist and pull sideways on the knob to gain entry. A staircase led down, lit by red lanterns. Smoke filled Kate's lungs, a sweet, heavy smell. *Oh, the air is poisonous in here.* When they reached the bottom of the stairs, another small man was waiting. *Is this the opium den master?* Wu made a sign, and the man nodded. He stood ogling Kate up and down for a moment, nodding slowly, then from an ornate table handed her a jar and a three-foot-long pipe crafted with a small metal bowl shaped like a covered cup with a hole in the centre. *Damn! He wants me to hold the pipes? Without gloves?* He guided her into a low, arched chamber far from the stairs and indicated a spot for her to stand. Wu had vanished. All around bodies were reclining on half-beds and pillows, dark, divided alcoves of European and Asian men. The smoke made everything cloudy, the light from the lanterns was dim and ruddy, and small open-flame lamps were burning throughout the cellar.

"Pipe, pipe," a voice muttered weakly from the darkness.

The den master waved Kate over and demonstrated how to pass the pipe, helping the customer to hold it. Opening the jar he withdrew a thin metal spatula with black putty on the end. Kate glanced in the container and saw something that looked like thick currant jam. *God's wounds, I'm holding a jar of opium?* She watched as he applied the narcotic to the orifice of the pipe bowl. He then took up one of the small lamps and fired the putty. As it started to burn he poked it through the hole with the other end of the spatula. The customer inhaled deeply, clutching the pipe with both hands. The den master then led Kate back to the table and gave her another pipe, the ivory mouthpiece stained brown. She held it, the jar in her other hand, wishing she could set them down and merely observe the wretched business from a corner.

Another voice called from a nearby couch. Kate approached the addict and followed the procedure, but fumbled a bit and inhaled when she lit the opium, causing her throat to burn and eyes to water, then immediately after the man exhaled into her face as well. *How horrible! Why do people do this?* The man motioned with his hand for more, and he took six doses before Kate could back away, feeling light-headed. From then on she was particularly careful to hold her breath when she fired the putty.

Each time she distributed a pipe, Kate returned to the ornate table and collected another. She noticed several other girls in blue outfits, appearing momentarily out of the smoke and shadows in other parts of the cellar, carrying pipes and jars. More customers entered, but they were guided away from Kate for their first doses. The den master would occasionally stroll about picking up pipes from stupefied addicts and placing them back on the table. Some of the men would whisper, some would call out or laugh or weep. Many of them reached at Kate with vacant eyes, but she dodged their grasps. *These men seem quite disturbed.* After a while she could feel her head floating off her shoulders, grew extremely tired, and just wanted to lie down. Her stomach and throat hurt, and she realized that for long spells she was holding her breath, causing drowsiness. *Got to concentrate. I'm supposed to find out where Napier is ...*

Just as Kate handed off the latest pipe, the den master was

suddenly beside her. He had two pipes and led her to a dark alcove. Men in plain brown uniforms were lying within with groggy faces. *These must be a pair of Napier's men.* They were slurring to each other as Kate perched beside them to prepare a pipe, getting the opium and lamp ready. She leaned in to hear better. They were speaking Portuguese. *Oh no, that's not one of my stronger languages.* Listening intently, her mind muddled, she did understand mention of "the King" several times. Passing off the pipes, manipulating the spatula and lamp, she gave each man three doses. She heard them murmur something about "two days' time at the river fort" and "very important."

Kate tried to rise but swooned, sitting down again. *Oh, my head ...* She set down the jar and rubbed her temples, then discerned a pull on her hair. She lay back and felt weightless as the men dragged her slowly into the alcove. Hands ran down her body, caressing her shoulders, sides, and hips. *No, you shouldn't do that ... but does it really matter?* She rolled over and lay on them for a moment, not certain what was happening, her usually active mind lost in a fog. *This feels nice. I could have a little nap.* A hand started to clumsily stroke her buttocks. *Wait ... don't let the men touch you.*

Kate found she had no strength, her head oddly detached from her body, but then focused. Pushing up with all her will she backed out of their grip and left them clutching the pipes. *I've got to get out of here. Where's Wu?* She tried to find the exit, but it seemed as though her eyes were floating away from her body. Pitching forward, she fell on the stairs. *I could sleep here on the floor.* Half crawling, she pulled herself up to the black door. Someone opened it for her, and she stumbled out into the passage, fresh cool air filling her lungs. Kate took deep breaths trying to regain her balance, noticing she couldn't feel the breeze on her skin. *Something's really wrong with me. I don't feel at all like myself.*

Firm arms wrapped around her shoulders and back and led her out of the dark passage and into the moonlit alley. Glancing to her left she saw Colonel Bob's profile and bushy whiskers, then to the right her grandfather. By the time they reached the *Otter*, Kate found her mind cleared and senses returned. She shivered in the cold, but the night was actually warm and humid. Feeling extremely tired she collapsed under several blankets and fell into a deep sleep.

⁜

When Kate awoke, daylight streamed in the cabin porthole, and she felt a great deal better. The previous night was blurry, but she remembered what Napier's men had said. Taking off the Chinese outfit, she put on a green walking suit, proceeded to the galley, and found Mrs. Farewell having breakfast with some of the crew. Joining them, she enjoyed a hearty meal, then went on deck.

"You all right, girl?" Colonel Bob asked as she approached.

"Yes, I'm fine. You're aware of what's going on?"

"I filled him in, Kate," Sir Tom said with a shrug. "You needn't worry, we're both old soldiers. We had to follow you last night."

"Of course, I'm glad you did. Thank you, gentlemen. I was in a bad way."

"Now what?"

"I've got to go see Wu. I have a few questions for him, and we need to exchange clothes."

Feeling confident enough to make the visit on her own, Kate bundled up the outfit and made her way to the back door of the silk storeroom. On entering she saw Wu delivering another tirade to the workers, sending them to various aisles. She waited for him to finish before drawing near. When the foreman saw her he scurried over, took the bundle, and stowed it under a counter. He brought out a very neat package of brown paper tied with string and handed it to Kate.

"What did you find out, Lotus Blossom?"

"Would Mr. Napier be referred to as the king?"

"Napier? King?"

I'll take that as a maybe. "I believe he's coming, or meeting someone, with something important tomorrow," she said, hoping to prompt the little man. "They mentioned a river fort. Do you have any idea whither it is?"

Wu stared at Kate with unblinking cloudy brown eyes for a moment.

"Fort up Bei Jiang, north river."

"Why would he be at this fort?"

"If he there it must be slaves. He buy girls."

"Girls? What do you mean? I thought it was the opium addicts who became slaves."

"No. Addicts sell their daughters to get more opium."

"How old are these girls?" *I think I'm going to see red.*

"Ten, eleven, twelve."

"He is a devil!" Kate felt her body tense, fists clenching, teeth grinding. *Grrr! My poor little sisters! I wish I could be like Nemesis, remorseless and vengeful, with wings and a fiery sword.*

"You kill him?"

"No, but I will arrange his arrest. My grandfather will bring the blackguard in and turn him over to the British authorities. We'll ensure he returns to England for trial."

"Bring him in? Trial?" Wu made the bad smell face again, scrunching up his nose and mouth.

"Yes. He won't trouble you, or your people, ever again."

"I make arrangements. Meet me at Thirteen Factories Street city gate when sun come up tomorrow."

Kate left the New English Factory in high dudgeon. *The outrage. I think I'm going to burst. My head hurts.* She tore off her hat and threw her hair around wildly, not caring what people might think. *I've got to let the heat out.* Feeling somewhat ill, Kate stormed back to the *Otter. I've got to calm down. We have to look after Henry.*

✜

Kate, Mrs. Farewell, Sir Tom, Colonel Bob, and three crewmen went to the infirmary to collect Henry and his possessions. She had brought her temper under control, and tied her hair away from her face with a ribbon. The sick doctor was quite delirious when placed on a litter for transport. Several staff came to the door to wish him a safe journey.

Down on the waterfront, where the Royal Navy sailors were waiting with a launch, Kate took a moment to lean over the litter and examine the young man's features.

"I'll see you in Bombay, Henry Tattersall." She glanced around, but then ignored everyone and placed a soft kiss on his forehead. "That's my first kiss to you," she whispered. "You owe me the same, when we meet again." Then, moving aside, Kate stood blinking tears while he was loaded.

Mrs. Farewell put an arm around her. The launch moved off, the sailors plying their oars, and was soon lost in the maze of little boats and ships filling the river. Kate turned into the arms of her old nanny and wept bitterly.

That afternoon, moping around on deck, puffy-eyed and weepy, Kate stood in a light rain not caring about getting wet. *I must stop wallowing in despair. Henry will be all better when I see him. Yes, and we'll go sightseeing in Bombay together. Then maybe we'll have our genuine first kiss. Now I need to concentrate on Wish Napier. I hope it isn't raining tomorrow.* Looking out at the shore she spotted Sir Tom striding along, splashing through the muddy puddles, with a parcel.

He waved, and called, "Your new clothes. Breeches and jacket, all done. I bought a pair of straps for you, too."

Kate went to her cabin and tried them on, not minding at all that it was a man's suit. The riding pants were tapered, brought in by eight buttons on the outside seam of each leg, and ended a little below the knees, designed to be worn suspended by straps, but she found her hips adequate to hold them up. The jacket came to the top of her thighs, had four patch pockets, two breast and two hip, and a built-in belt at the waist. She couldn't believe the seam-stresses had altered a suit so quickly. They'd done an outstanding job, and it fit quite well.

Kate peered at herself in the mirror. *Won't Napier be surprised to see me in these clothes. When I confront him about the slaves, he'll be so ashamed of himself, the disgrace he's bringing to his family, I'm sure his code of honour will prevail. Grandfather will give him a good talking-to, then we'll bring him back here. I shall carry out this ... this tasking!*

ALONG THE BEI JIANG

Kate rose in the darkness prior to dawn and padded silently from the cabin she shared with Mrs. Farewell. She had placed everything she thought would be needed in the engine room the night before. Taking up the lantern burning in the galley, she lit a candle and tiptoed to her supplies. Her new outfit slipped on comfortably over silk hose, long stockings, a linen shirt, and the vest from her riding habit. *I'm glad I don't have to do this in a pretty gown.* Kate then tied and buckled the tall buff boots she'd brought lest the need arise for travelling by horse, but had thus far used only on the camel caravan and rainy days.

Quickly she plaited her hair over each ear, feeling it was the best way to keep her long, unruly tresses under control. Taking out the protective goggles Jack had given her, Kate strapped them around the crown of her wide-brimmed canvas hat and put it low on her head. Fastening the belt and holster around her hips, she played with the fit for a moment, adjusting for the weight of the pistol. *This weapon probably saved our lives against those pirates, scaring them from entering the cabin.* She took the pistol in hand, checked it was loaded properly, and holstered it again.

Finally, she placed straps over both shoulders, one a sword belt with a thin sabre and one a canteen, and slipped on her brown leather riding gloves. Kate picked up the case housing the long-range rifle and a bag of ammunition for her pistol. *This is rather awkward; there must be a better way to carry all this. I don't even have a handbag.*

With no time allotted to alter her kit, she merely pushed the canteen back behind her pistol then stepped carefully along the hall and up the ladder. Her grandfather stood waiting in his beige cotton suit, smoking a pipe, a sword on his hip and a gun cradled in his arm.

"All ready?" he whispered.

"Yes. Here's the rifle. Why do you want it?"

"The telescope will be useful." He took the case from her. "And surely we'll find time today to put it together. Maybe do some shooting in the countryside."

"All right, but I'll let you try it. Every time I fire it I get a bruised shoulder and a black eye."

The gangplank was pulled in for the night, but, dressed in their field suits and boots, they easily jumped from the rail down to the logs which served as a dock. The factories were quiet, and the grey of dawn revealed only a few labourers who moved about the streets as they hurried to the rendezvous. Kate spied Wu waiting in his usual faded outfit and cap, tapping his pointer impatiently on his foot. As they approached he scurried off, so she had to jog to keep him in sight. The Chinese soldiers standing sentry remained stationary as she passed. With her sword and pistol flapping uncomfortably, Kate didn't catch him until they were deep into the city, Sir Tom well behind but matching Wu's pace and never out of view. Gongs started to ring out. At first only a couple, the tone clear and separate, then dozens mingling together, then hundreds, and an accompanying rumble as the multitudinous populace rose for a new day.

Finally, at a gate in a stone wall, Wu stopped and Sir Tom strode up.

"This my grandfather," Kate began, "Sir Thomas Ro—"

"Do not tell me his name!" Wu growled. "I will call him White Crane. This way."

He led them to a yard where horses were gathered in small groups.

"Pick one." Wu waved his stick at the animals.

Putting down her case and ammunition, Kate sidled over to a group of ponies and stood still. A roan mare with a white face moved towards her.

"Nice girl," she cooed. "Would you like to come with me?" Glancing the animal over and seeing she was sound, Kate patted her neck and let the solid little horse smell her hair. Looking around she saw Wu in a straw sun hat, standing by with a bridle and blanket, a donkey already saddled waiting behind him.

"Lotus Blossom, you are a horsewoman."

"Thank you." She eased the bit into the mare's mouth. "How far do we have to go?"

"Most of morning ride, then you see." Wu brought out a battered cavalry saddle.

"That's a good fit for me," Kate observed, examining the pommel, seat, and cantle. "It must have been crafted for small troopers. But I wonder if there's a sidesaddle in the shed?"

Wu pursed his lips and blinked. He held out the saddle and shook it at her.

"Yes, all right, never mind." Kate took the saddle and laid it on the pony. *I'm wearing breeches anyway, I may as well ride like a man — it's how I've raced many times. What would Nanny say?* She quickly buckled the girth and started adjusting the stirrup leathers.

Sir Tom was quick to tack up, selecting a tall bay gelding, using spare straps to secure the rifle case to the back of his saddle.

Wu watched him. "You have rifle in box?"

"Yes, we may try it out today," Sir Tom replied, climbing into his saddle. "It has a powerful spyglass, so when we get near the fort, show it to us from far away. That way we can scan the area and see if Napier is present."

Wu raised his eyebrows, blinked a few times, peered at the box, and cocked his head, but didn't say another word as he climbed on his donkey.

✣

The sun just cleared the horizon as they left Canton, crossed several bridges, and followed a muddy lane into a rolling plain, the river visible on their right. The countryside grew quieter the farther they rode from the city, and by mid-morning it seemed they had left civilization behind. Occasionally a heavily loaded native trudged by, bent over and head down, probably making for the busy markets at the coast. The day turned warm and dry. Close to noon, when Kate was wishing she'd brought some food, Wu left the lane and coaxed his donkey into a valley, dismounting by a grove of trees.

"I show you fort," the little old man said softly.

Securing their animals in the shade where they could graze, the men utilized a patch of bushes to relieve themselves, while Kate hid and did the same. They then followed Wu up a steep slope to a hilltop, stopping near the crest. In the distance, past several lower hills and trees, stood a walled compound about the size of a square acre with horses inside. One large gate lay open towards their position, and along the river several little boats were pulled up on the sand. At each corner of the fort there was a squat building, and it all appeared to be made of mud. About a dozen men were visible.

"You need go closer?" Wu jabbed at the stronghold with his pointer.

"How about we get out the spyglass and have a look?" Sir Tom suggested. "See if we spot Napier, then we'll come up with a contingency plan."

"I'll get it," Kate declared, feeling excited.

She slid down the slope, untied the rifle case from the gelding, carried it to a log lying nearby, and took out the telescope, hands trembling a bit.

This is it. I'm having a great adventure! Stay calm, stay calm. She scrambled back up the slope and sighted on the fort, adjusting the eyepiece. The sun reflected off the mud walls, forcing her to squint, then she remembered the goggles. She removed her hat and put the protective lenses in place. She noticed her grand-father and Wu watching silently, standing near the top of the hill, following her progress. *Let's see, where's Napier?* Kate looked from man to man, and could see many different skin tones and racial features clearly. The smoky yellow tint of the lenses took away the sun's glare perfectly, just as it had in the desert. The men all wore the same rough brown uniform and were armed with various weapons. *Hmm, where is Napier?* She eased onto one knee, adjusting her sabre, trying to steady the telescope, exam-ining faces more carefully. She scanned for a bit, but none of the men resembled Napier. *I wish my stomach would stop growling.*

"Let me have a look," Sir Tom said quietly.

Kate jumped, startled by his voice. He had knelt beside her, but she was so intent on searching she hadn't noticed. She passed over the telescope and her goggles.

"Are your eyes still sharp?" Kate asked.

"Not bad for an old man. This is longer and thinner than I expected," he said while twisting the eyepiece.

"It runs about three-quarters the length of the barrel, and has two mounts. It really is quite ingenious."

"Focusing is easy enough, but how do you adjust the rifle for distance?"

"Oh, you estimate how far the target is, then turn a knob on the front mount, so there is some guesswork."

"Keep looking." He passed the telescope and goggles back. "Let me know if Napier makes an appearance. I want to have a few words with Wu. You don't mind letting a couple of old men rest in the shade for a bit, do you?"

"No, of course not."

Kate watched as men arrived or departed in their little boats, and others trotted in on horseback. It had been nearly half an hour when there was some shouting that caught her attention.

On a trail winding into the hills a gang of men appeared, and with them in a row were about a score of girls. *Oh my God, this must be the slaves. And they do look about twelve years old!* The men all began moving around, and several more came from the buildings. Kate checked each face, searching for Napier to no avail. *Perhaps he isn't here?*

Suddenly, among all the brown uniforms, she spotted a man in shiny red and yellow robes striding confidently to the middle of the compound. He was dressed like some kind of Chinese nobleman with gold trim throughout his clothing glittering as he moved. When he turned, Kate saw a long moustache and goatee, rouge, and thick black eye paint, then beneath it all the face of Aloysius James Napier. *So this is the king? Oh, Wish, what have you become? How did you turn so evil?*

Kate got to her feet, pushed her goggles up onto her forehead, and jumped down the slope, finding Wu standing, her grandfather sitting on the log, the assembled rifle across his lap. *Why did he put it together? Did he ...?* The old soldier's face was set with stony determination, a somewhat tired expression around his eyes.

"He's there," Kate said, feeling dread creep into her breast. "And the slaves are being brought from the west. What are you doing? Aren't we going to ride in and talk to him?"

"Wu and I have been chatting," Sir Tom said quietly. "He says we'd probably be gunned down before we made it to the front gate."

"Really?" Kate let her eyes go from her grandfather to Wu and back again. "Shouldn't we try?"

"And if we did, and managed to confront Napier, do you truly believe he would give up his little kingdom?"

"I'm not certain. I ... I thought you were going to remind him of duty, and family honour."

"His men would cut me to ribbons, and you would be his plaything."

"You don't know that." Kate's words sounded hollow in her own head, but she pressed on. "Perhaps he would —"

"Shall I spell out every detail?" Sir Tom said sharply, getting to his feet. "You'd be better off dead than in his bed, then God knows what after."

"Please don't talk like that, Grandfather," Kate whispered, her vision blurring, a hot tear rolling down her cheek. It was like he was a different man, the hard soldier beneath the loving grandparent.

"Right then, time for action. Are you going to help me make this shot?"

Kate glanced up at the trees. *The leaves are still, barely moving, there's hardly a breath of wind. Yes, the hill would be a good place to shoot from, about seven or eight hundred yards? It'll be a long shot ...*

"Katelyn! Are you prepared to do this?"

"Yes." Kate nodded and wiped the tears from her face. "Here, let me mount the telescope, and I'll adjust the front knob to eight."

They scrambled up the slope, and Kate reluctantly, but quickly, got into a prone position, Sir Tom lying beside her. *I have to do this ... this is for the good of our Empire, but it still hurts ...* She picked out Napier near the middle of the compound, talking to several men. The girls were outside the gate, standing obediently in a line. She sighted down the telescope, adjusted the focus, then passed the rifle to her grandfather, along with her goggles. *Oh, Wish, why? How? How did you become this? Your poor parents.*

"He's the only one in bright clothes, dressed like an emperor," she said, watching Sir Tom set three bullets on the ground between them. "The propellant Jack uses for those creates hardly any smoke, so our position won't be given away. Open the lever," she instructed, laying her head down, hiding under her hat. "Now put the round in from the top, that's it, the little cover hinges in. Slide the cartridge right into the barrel chamber. Close the lever, cock the hammer, you're ready to shoot."

"Isn't there a percussion cap?"

"No," Kate sighed, an ache throbbing in her breast and head. "It's built into the bottom of the cartridge casing."

Out of the corner of her eye she watched him adjust the eye-piece slightly, then settle into a slow breathing pattern, preparing to fire. "Aim high on his breast, then if there is a bit more drop it'll still hit his stomach or groin. Whatever, he won't survive."

Kate waited, and felt dizzy. *I've got to steady my breathing. Remember, he deserves it. Come then, Grandfather, get it over with ...*

The crack of the gunshot almost made Kate jump out of her skin, every muscle tensing. She sprang to her feet and stood in a crouched position. Sir Tom struggled up, passing her the rifle and goggles, then holding his cheekbone.

"Ensure I was accurate," he ordered, while the sound of distant shots started ringing out.

Kate managed to assess the situation while pulling on her goggles. Men were running and ducking in all directions, and the girls ran back up the trail. *Hurrah! They're getting away!* She steadied the weapon and peered down the telescope. Napier lay motionless, a heap of gaudy clothing. A few men fired blind out the gate. She lowered the rifle and turned to her grandfather, who had moved back by Wu.

"You got him."

Wu immediately started hopping down the slope, calling over his shoulder, "Shoot some more, Lotus Blossom. Scare the men. It give us more time to get away!"

Yes, and for the girls to escape, too! Kate knelt and took up a round, loaded, and aimed at a bucket close to several men gathered behind a low wall. She took a slow breath, let it out halfway ... *Steady ... Fire!* The rifle kicked viciously into Kate's shoulder and banged her cheekbone. Actually stunned a bit from the recoil, seeing stars fluttering around her head, she reloaded and tried to aim.

"Let's go," her grandfather called.

Kate shot into the open gateway, hitting the ground, feeling her shoulder jerk, the pain stabbing deeply, and her face go numb. She sighted once more, seeing the men cowering, shooting harmlessly into the forest. The girls were gone from view. She turned and leapt from the hill, landing almost at the bottom of the slope, and sprinted to the log, stopping at the rifle case.

"Leave it," Sir Tom said, mounting up. "Just take the ammunition."

"You ride back to Canton quick," Wu yelled. "Wait at horse yard."

"What will you do?" Kate slid her goggles down around her neck and put bullets in her pockets. She thought there should be at least a few minutes' time for an escape. The men wouldn't know where the shots came from, and would probably be keeping their heads down. More cracks of gunfire echoed in the distance.

"I take other trail!" Wu moved like a much younger man as he crossed the low ground, climbed on his donkey, and disappeared into the trees.

"Take my pistol and bag of cartridges," Kate said to her grandfather. "They're the usual paper kind. And there's a tin of percussion caps in there as well. It would be better than your single-shot gun if we run into trouble."

"All right." Sir Tom took the weapon and threw the belt over his shoulder.

Kate climbed into the saddle, cradling the rifle. "I'm ready!"

They kicked up to a canter and rode out of the valley onto the lane, then broke into a gallop. Kate's heart had been racing, her actions frantic, but she began to calm. Taking stock, she realized her hat and canteen were missing, left behind in the rush. Sir Tom's mount, bigger with longer legs, outpaced Kate's pony quickly, but the little mare seemed to have a great deal of stamina.

I wonder if any men are coming this way yet? Perhaps they're still hiding in the fort. We can't gallop all the way to Canton. Watching her grandfather pulling back to a canter up ahead, Kate slowed as well and tried listening for any indication she was being followed.

She quickly came to the conclusion that unless she actually stopped it would be hard to hear anything lower than a yell or a shot, so slowed to a walk. Immediately she perceived hoofbeats. Coaxing the pony into a gallop again, she leaned forward as a shot rang out behind her. The lane came to a wide open valley. *They'll have clear view of us through there!*

"Go straight for the hills, Kate!" Sir Tom yelled, veering to the right.

Halfway across the space several shots boomed behind her. *Please don't hit my horse.* Kate feared for the pony, knowing the men might aim at the largest target. Bending close to the animal's neck, she kicked boot heels into her flanks, urging greater speed. Shots sounded on the left and right. *Oh no, they got ahead of me! I'm done for!*

Expecting to feel a round tear into her at any moment, Kate still rode on desperately, almost dropping the rifle and nearly losing the reins because of trembling hands, trying to reach the low hills ahead. Shots were still going off, but it seemed the tone had changed. Glancing over her shoulder, she saw none of the pursuers entering the open area. *I must be out of range, why are they still shooting?* Getting safely around the first hill, she pulled to a halt and dismounted. Charging to the top of the grassy mound, she levered open the rifle and tore a cartridge from her pocket. Lying down and loading, she skimmed the edges of the valley with the telescope. Along the lane, directly opposite her position, were the men who'd been chasing her, shooting to their left and right. Looking to both flanks, Kate spied men on each, firing and reloading as fast as they could. *Colonel Bob! And some of the crew! They covered my retreat, I must return the favour.* She could see her grandfather in a dangerously close position, using her pistol effectively.

Aiming across the opening, she picked a target, a tree branch by a man's head, and fired. The kick pushed her back, adding to the pain in her shoulder and cheek. Not bothering to check whether she'd found the mark or not, she reloaded and fired again. She hit the ground a few times, kicking up sand. As fast as she could, reload and fire, until her bullets were spent. Using the telescope to scan the trees, Kate perceived shadowy movement. *They're moving to the flanks through the forest.* She looked for her grandfather. He was mounted, and riding south with some of the men. She checked the other crewmen, and they were doing the same with Colonel Bob. Shots started again, Napier's men aiming from the forest. *Time to flee!* Kate rose and started running down the hill.

Almost at the same moment, a man rode from the lane and halted by Kate's pony. He dismounted, draped his hat on his pommel, and turned, fixing steely eyes on Kate.

"What's all this, then?" Cavanagh asked with his slightly amused expression.

"I don't have time to chat," Kate said breezily, painfully aware shots were being fired across the valley. *He must have been coming from the city and doesn't know what's happened. Why isn't he reacting to the gunfire?*

"Are you the cause of all that rumpus, sweet lady?" The Irishman moved closer, cocking his head to listen, eyes boring in at Kate's clothes and rifle. He put a monocle in place, his low brow and prominent cheekbones ideal for such an eyepiece, and studied the rifle. "What kind of a gun have you got there?"

"It's nothing, just something my brother made." She started getting agitated. *I don't have time for acting nonchalant.* "It doesn't work."

"It looks extraordinary, and smells like it worked recently." He stood directly in front of her now. "I think you better come with me."

Kate set down the rifle and drew her sword, tossing away the belt and sheath. Cavanagh took a quick step back, his crooked smile vanishing.

"I have to go," Kate said forcefully. "Get out of my way."

In a fluid motion his long cavalry sabre was drawn from its heavy bronze scabbard and rang off the light sword, almost knocking it from the Kate's grip. She hopped sideways, recovered, parried, and lunged. Cavanagh beat her blade aside, slashed back at her hip, then aimed a neat thrust at her face, holding his scabbard expertly as a low guard.

Eek! He could have cut me both times. He's playing with me. I've got to get away from here. Kate tried a series of feints and thrusts, only to be countered at each attempt.

Finally she lunged high. Cavanagh blocked her blade and pushed it up over her head, then stepped into her, letting go of his scabbard and wrapping his free arm around the small of her back. He pulled her close so they were crushed together like dancers embracing.

"That's a lovely outfit, so it is," the Irishman said in his casual lilt, as though they hadn't been duelling at all. "I believe we use the same tailor, Mrs. Tattersall."

"Oh, yes." Kate noticed how strongly he held her, his piercing eyes and lopsided smile. "They do look the same."

She slid her blade down and awkwardly hacked the man on the forehead. Blood erupted from the wound, filling his right eye as he reeled back, cutting his weapon down and across with lightning speed and overpowering force. Kate jumped away, her sabre torn from her grip. She bent and grabbed the rifle by the barrel and brought it around with all her might, catching Cavanagh on the shoulder with the butt, sending blood splashing across his face. The mercenary stumbled and tried to wipe the gore from his eyes.

Cradling the rifle, Kate ran to her pony and mounted. She turned and glanced back at the Irishman for just a moment, then scanned the surrounding area. To the west a man on a donkey was silhouetted on a hilltop for a heartbeat, then he was gone. Kate kicked into a gallop and headed south, pushing the little mare until the next valley. It was quiet; no more shots rang out. Relief washed over her when she saw Sir Tom and the crewmen galloping in her direction.

"Ha ha!" Colonel Bob bellowed. "Good show! Proper little battle!"

Kate couldn't help but smile and wave. *Ow! I've bruised my shoulder again. Oh pooh, I'll have a black eye later ...*

CANTON, AND THE CHINESE COAST

When Kate and the men reached the city, they returned Colonel Bob's and the crew's horses first, then proceeded to the yard where Wu had hired Kate's and Sir Tom's mounts. Disassembling the rifle, they wrapped it in a piece of sackcloth to keep it from the view of curious eyes. Waiting for some time, and seeing the sun in decline, they gave up on the little man appearing and strolled back through Canton. Colonel Bob explained how he had followed them on Sir Tom's orders, not sure what they were going to do or how they could help. It had been quite difficult for them to pass through the restricted streets and hire horses, then find their way along the river, drawing near only as the shooting started. Kate walked between Sir Tom and Colonel Bob, arm in arm, going over what had happened and thanking them for everything. The crewmen strode along behind, singing campaign songs. Chinese soldiers, obviously surprised to find an odd, inharmonious party of elderly Britons in the city, remained calm and followed at a safe distance.

"I'm glad that's over," Kate declared.

"How do you feel?" Sir Tom asked.

"All right, thank you. I'm still confused by how I ended up with this ... this tasking. How it fits together with Jack and Foreign Affairs." Kate gave each of them a little pull on the elbows. "You must keep all this a secret."

"We've been in service to the Crown all our lives," Sir Tom said. "You needn't worry about us. And the crew don't know what it was all about."

"Who was this fellow you duelled with again?" Colonel Bob queried.

"An Irishman," she answered. "Mercenary, said his name's Cavanagh."

"And a Royal Engineer?"

"That's what he said. Probably a liar."

"There was such a fellow made a baronet, hero of the Afghan War in 'thirty-nine."

"Truly? It cannot be the same person. It must have been someone else."

"Likely," Colonel Bob agreed. "The British Army is full of Irish and Scots. Some names appear over a hundred times in the same regiment."

"Oh yes, interesting." *I'm not really concerned with such matters.* "Now, I have to purchase a new hat ..."

Upon reaching the factories they could see an inky cloud starting to rise from the warehouses on the other side of the creek. As the smell of the smoke wafted around them, Kate recognized it instantly from her experience in the opium den. Running ahead of the men to the creek she saw the building she had visited with Wu, the one which housed Napier's goods, roaring into flame. Chinese labourers formed bucket brigades and were dousing the nearby structures, but letting that warehouse burn. It was clearly organized, and Kate searched for Wu but couldn't spot him. She felt gladdened to see the destruction, but worried what fate lay in store for the peasant girls she'd seen at the fort. *Where will they go? Someday, there won't be slavery.* With that hope on her mind Kate hurried to the *Otter* in time for dinner.

⁘

The next morning they put out along the coast. There were four stops to make and images to be created. Compared to the adventures of the last few days, Kate found the exercise rather dull. She felt no apprehension while casually examining the new foreign buildings and surreptitiously capturing their images. The crates of Bibles were delivered to the Anglican Mission at Ningpo, and at Shanghai the camera plates were almost spent.

There were long hours to relive everything she had done and experienced, and it all thrilled her to the very core. Sometimes Kate would think about the men she'd seen killed, in particular the young pirate and Napier. It hurt her heart when she considered taking away someone's life, but she told herself it was necessary, fate forcing her hand or in the name of justice.

Returning to Canton they prepared for their voyage west, loaded with various supplies and at full capacity with coal and water. While the boat was being looked after, Kate took the opportunity to see if Wu had surfaced. In her green walking suit, dust swirling around her skirt, she made the now familiar stroll to the silk store-room at the New English Factory. When she entered, the harangue of the ancient man assailed her ears. He badgered a labourer and waved his pointer in all directions. When Wu saw Kate he stopped short, and even smiled just faintly.

"Hello, Mr. Wu," she called musically, smiling brightly, genuinely happy to see him.

"Hello to you, miss," he barked and bowed.

Kate noticed he didn't correct her use of an honorific. *Hmm, why not call me Lotus Blossom?* "I'm glad you're all right." She drew close. "Were you responsible for the fire?"

"No, of course not." Wu waved his pointer back and forth erratically and shook his head, but had a small knowing curl to his lips.

"I'm leaving for India tomorrow." *We don't have much to say. After all that.*

"I have gift for you," the old man announced.

He scurried down a counter and brought out something of blue fabric. Kate thought at first he carried the outfit she'd worn to the opium den, but when Wu paraded it close she could see it had the shine of a new garment, padded and embroidered. He held it up for her to examine. The gift was a short robe of bright blue silk, absolutely exquisite, and the intricate colourful stitching made it appear almost magical. A dragon, in dozens of shades of green, red, and gold, breathing smoke, coiled up the left breast. The hours it must have taken to produce such art was beyond Kate's imagination. She took off her gloves and jacket, something she wouldn't normally do in public, put on the robe, and did up the little knotted fasteners; it fit perfectly. Then she took off her hat and tossed out her hair, letting it fall around her shoulders. Admiring the craftsmanship, running her hands over the glossy soft fabric, she glanced up beaming and saw Wu had tears in his eyes.

"Oh, Mr. Wu." Kate felt tears forming as well, her eyelashes wet. "It's beautiful beyond words. I'm so honoured."

"No, it is I who am honoured," he insisted, cuffing a drop off his nose.

"I have to ask ..." Kate could feel tears flowing down her cheeks. "Why this?" She gingerly touched the embroidery. "Why not lotus blossoms?"

"You are like flower," Wu pronounced firmly. "But even more, you are a fierce dragon lady!"

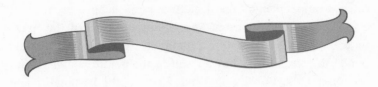

EPILOGUE

The trip to India being uneventful, Kate found time to reflect. She told everyone her main concern was reaching Bombay, to care for Henry and see him safely home. Although she didn't put it into words, she hoped a courtship might follow. Then, perhaps, an engagement and wedding.

However, in the evenings, Kate would put on her Chinese robe, stand on deck, let the wind blow through her hair, and almost wish some pirates would attack. She would visit the boat's armoury and try holding the different weapons, or put the rifle together just to take it apart again; it was a shame she had lost the case. Although there hadn't been an occasion for her to fire the revolving pistol since her first battle, Sir Tom had used it to great effect, and she still cleaned the weapon, reloaded it, and wore it under her skirt a few times pretending to be a some kind of covert operative.

Only a few months earlier, Kate hadn't known she was capable of such deeds. Had she changed? She didn't think so. Having spent a childhood dreaming of travel and adventure, pretending to be a wild corsair or daring despatch rider, it still proved something of a shock to know she'd participated in two clandestine taskings for the British Secret Service. There were still lots of questions that needed answers: How was Henry involved? Could Jack have known of the danger? Did Palmerston presume she would act as an executioner for him?

Kate felt quietly proud of carrying out the taskings with such courage and aplomb. She'd captured the images of the new construction, taken care of Napier, and out-duelled Cavanagh to make good her escape. Admittedly, her grandfather had pulled the trigger that put an end to the opium smuggler, but they had worked as a team, and defeating the Irishman might have been because her charm caught him off guard. It all led to more questions: Perhaps being a young lady gave her a certain advantage? Was this something Palmerston had surmised when they met? Might all the Secret Service taskings take the operatives into dangerous situations where swordplay and marksmanship would be required to survive?

Whatever the answers, Kate knew she wasn't really an operative, and she was more concerned with becoming Mrs. Dr. Henry Tattersall. And Kate Tattersall she would be, but a British Secret Service clandestine operative as well, the next adventure waiting in India.

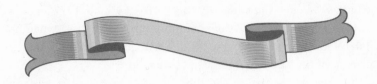

AUTHOR'S NOTE

The First Opium War was the result of trade disputes and diplomatic squabbling between China under the Qing Dynasty and the British Empire after the Emperor attempted to halt illegal opium trafficking. Opium was smuggled by merchants from India (under British taxation and government control) into China in defiance of the Emperor's prohibition laws. A Chinese citizen found in possession of opium faced execution by beheading. Open warfare between Britain and China broke out in 1839, lasting until 1842, with Palmerston serving as Secretary for Foreign Affairs. China was defeated, leaving the Emperor having to tolerate the opium smuggling and suffering an immeasurable loss of respect. Britain forced the Chinese government into signing the Treaty of Nanking, which included the opening of four additional ports to unrestricted foreign trade. Many Chinese people found the agreements humiliating, and these sentiments contributed to the Taiping Rebellion (1850–1864), the Second Opium War (1856–1860), and the Boxer Rebellion (1899–1901), in which millions of lives were lost, making nineteenth-century European and American wars seem insignificant by comparison. The vast majority of British citizens had no idea how much wealth was generated by the opium trade, or how it had a great deal to do with the building of their Empire; it was a very dark chapter of English history.

✤

Charles Douglas-Compton (26 May 1816–3 March 1877), was a British peer, styled Earl Compton from birth until 1851 when he inherited the title 3rd Marquess of Northampton. He served as a trustee of the National Gallery in London.

Charles Augustus Bennet, 6th Earl of Tankerville (10 January 1810–18 December 1899), styled Lord Ossulston between 1822 and 1859, was a British peer and Conservative politician. He married Lady Olivia Montagu (18 July 1830–15 February 1922), eldest daughter of George Montagu, 6th Duke of Manchester, at Kimbolton Castle, Huntingdonshire, on 29 January 1850. They had five children.

Spencer Joshua Alwyne Compton, 2nd Marquess of Northampton (2 January 1790–17 January 1851), was a British nobleman and patron of science and the arts. From 1820–22 he was president of the Geological Society of London. He served as president of the Archaeological Institute of Great Britain and Ireland from 1845–46 and 1850–51, and president of the Royal Society from 1838–48; the dinosaur species *Regnosaurus northampton* was named after him. He held the position of president of the Royal Society of Literature from 1849 until his death.

Richard Plantagenet Campbell Temple-Nugent-Brydges-Chandos-Grenville, 3rd Duke of Buckingham and Chandos (10 September 1823–26 March 1889), styled Marquess of Chandos from 1839 to 1861, was a British soldier, politician, and administrator of British colonies.

Henry William George Paget (9 December 1821–30 January 1880), was styled Lord Paget until 1854. He was Earl of Uxbridge between 1854 and 1869, and finally the 3rd Marquess of Anglesey. He was a British peer and Liberal politician serving in the House of Commons and then the House of Lords.

Louis-Jacques-Mandé Daguerre (18 November 1787–10 July 1851), was a French artist and physicist. Known as one of the fathers of photography, he invented a process of photography that was named after him. He was also an accomplished painter and took part in the development of the diorama theatre.

William-Adolphe Bouguereau (30 November 1825–19 August 1905), was a French artist who favoured traditionalist style. In his realistic genre paintings he sometimes adapted tales from mythology, creating interpretations of classical subjects, concentrating on the female form, often idealized. During his lifetime he was particularly popular in France and America.

Lieutenant Thomas Fletcher Waghorn (20 June 1800–7 January 1850) joined the British Navy at the age of twelve as a midshipman. He participated in the Napoleonic and First Burmese War. As a postal pioneer he developed a new route from Britain to India. His road overland through Egypt reduced the journey by about ten thousand miles. What had previously been a three-month journey around Africa was possible in thirty-five to forty-five days. A railway between Suez and Cairo was completed in 1858. A year later preliminary excavations were begun, and on 17 November 1869 the Suez Canal opened.

John Russell (18 August 1792–28 May 1878), known as Lord Russell, was an English Liberal politician who served twice as Prime Minister of the United Kingdom. A younger son of the 6th Duke of Bedford, he did not expect to inherit or amount to anything, but he was knighted for his service and made the 1st Earl Russell in 1861.

The Peninsula and Oriental Steam Navigation Company (The P & O) is a British shipping and logistics company that still operates today. Its roots go back to 1822, when a London ship broker and a sailor from the Shetland Isles formed a partnership to operate a shipping line between England, Spain, and Portugal. In 1835, a Dublin ship owner joined the business, and the three men started a regular steamer service. In 1837, the business won a contract from the British Admiralty to deliver mail to the Iberian Peninsula, and in 1840 they acquired a contract to deliver mail to Alexandria in Egypt. By 1843 they were providing mail service from Suez to Ceylon, Madras, and Calcutta. In 1845 the service to Penang and Singapore was established, and in 1848 it was extended to Hong Kong.

While operating in the South China Sea between 1843 and 1851, the Royal Navy captured or destroyed roughly 150 pirate junks. British warships sailed as far as Borneo to rout out the pirates, even landing marines to go ashore and destroy their lairs.

Rimfire ammunition was patented in 1831 by French gunsmith Louis Nicolas Auguste Flobert (1819–1894), but never evolved into practical use until 1845. He mass-produced small-calibre, low-velocity bullets for indoor target practice. Smith & Wesson famously used a .22 calibre rimfire round for their first revolver, in 1857. Rimfire ammunition was produced in several calibres during the mid-nineteenth century, the largest being the .58 Miller. The .22 calibre long rifle rimfire cartridge is still very popular today.

Guncotton (nitrocellulose) was developed by various chemists through the 1830s and 1840s, being put into practical use as an explosive and propellant by about 1847. The original compound, made of cotton treated with sulphuric acid and potassium nitrate, had approximately six times the gas generation of an equal volume of black powder, and therefore produced outstanding muzzle velocities with much less smoke and heat. It was very unstable, leading to catastrophic explosions.

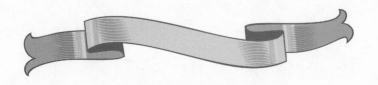

ABOUT THE AUTHOR

R.S. Fleming was born in Ottawa, Ontario, and has lived in Pierrefonds, Quebec, Mississauga, Ontario, Winnipeg, Manitoba, and Prince Edward County, Ontario. He served twenty-five years with the Canadian Forces in the infantry and as an instrument electrical and aviation technician. For his meritorious service in preserving the history and heritage of the RCAF he received the Queen's Diamond Jubilee Medal. Fleming is now an author, and *Kate Tattersall Adventures in China* is the first instalment of a ten part series.

Please visit katetattersall.com
to learn more.